RIVER TURTLE

Meet Clara Browning, a seventeen-year-old girl living in El Paso, Texas during the 1880's. Clara wants to ride in the seven day Mt. Franklin Race and become a veterinarian. Calling college a ridiculous idea for a girl and the race no place for a female, her father forbids both.

She secretly enters the race, hoping to win the race's purse to fund her education. Clara's best friend, Flash, an enormous pure white horse, carries her over the dangerous course.

In the mountains, the shocking secret of Flash's oddly shaped birthmark, which has haunted Clara for years, reveals itself. Shortly into the race, a mysterious stranger begins to help Clara. Although, he remains hidden, she knows he is always watching.

Through strange circumstances, her rival, Matthew Miller, an eighteen-year-old handsome rancher, also enters the race. Matthew must win the race to save his mother's ranch. He hates Clara because her father, El Paso's sheriff, had murdered Matthew's father many years earlier.

He becomes much more involved with Clara than ever anticipated. His resolve to stop her and her determination to win force them to use shocking methods against each other.

"I had dreams about that book, trying to guess what would happen next. I felt like reading the book all over again."
Nichole Blackshire **Steele Middle School, Muskegon, MI**

"I thought the book was one of the best books I've read in awhile." 8th grade student (name not given).
Lake Orion Middle School, Lake Orion, MI

"…I think that this book was sort of exciting because everything that happens is a surprise. William Horner
Steele Middle School, Muskegon, MI

While the events represented and some of the characters in this book may be based on actual historical events and real people, Clara Browning, Sheriff Browning, Matthew Miller, Ida Miller, Brewster Brothers, Unnamed Warrior, Jose', and all other characters are fictional characters, created by the Author.

Copyright 2000 by Cyndi Harper-Deiters
Library of Congress Card Number 00-091456
Printed in United States of America
ISBN 1-888831-00-6

River Turtle: Book One Clara Browning Series,
Cyndi Harper-Deiters

1. Railroad revolution Southwestern USA, 1883- **Young Adult Historical Fiction**
2. EL Paso Texas, 1883- **Light Romance-Fiction**
3. Mt. Franklin Race **Young Adult Adventure-Fiction**

Country Home Publishers:
6812 Old 28th St. Suite "J", SE Grand Rapids, MI 49546

COMING SOON

UNNAMED WARRIOR
BOOK TWO OF THE
CLARA BROWNING SERIES

PROJECTED RELEASE DATE
NOVEMBER 15, 2000

IOWA PASSAGE
BOOK THREE OF THE
CLARA BROWNING SERIES

PROJECTED RELEASE DATE
FEBRUARY 14, 2001

ADVANCE ORDERS AVAILABLE
BY CALLING COUNTRY HOME PUBLISHERS
AT 616-954-7634 OR FAXING
616-954-7633
OR
WRITING
COUNTRY HOME PUBLISHERS
6812 OLD 28TH ST., SE
SUITE "J"
GRAND RAPIDS, MI 49546
RESERVE YOUR COPY TODAY
FIRST 1000 COPIES SOLD OF BOOK TWO
AND THREE RECEIVE, FREE, A SPECIAL
GIFT FROM CYNDI HARPER-DEITERS

ACKNOWLEDGMENTS

Helen M. Bowers
Thank you, Helen, for the beautiful front cover painting and
your constant love and support in all of my endeavors.
Although Helen suffers from Macular Edema and Diabetic
Retinopathy disease causing her to be legally blind, she
continues to fulfill her life's destiny as an artist.

Jane Stroschin
Jane has the most beautiful soul in the Universe. My friend,
Jane, award winning artist, children's author, and book
illustrator, without a fee, painted the final small details on the
front cover as a gift for Helen and me.

Robert Ruggles and Grace Ruggles
Editors, mentors, and friends. I cannot thank them enough
for the many hours they worked on
River Turtle.

Norbert and Dawn Zimpfer
My new friends who own a very unique store called
` **Tabalooga** at 1049 28th St., SW Grand Rapids, MI Because of
their joint efforts and determination to find supreme quality,
we have hand carved, stone necklaces crafted exclusively for
RIVER TURTLE that will accompany the first 2000 copies
sold.

RIVER
TURTLE

BOOK ONE OF
THE CLARA BROWNING SERIES

Cyndi Harper-Deiters

For Ruby

You can make a

Difference!

Cyndi Harper-De.

10/3/2000

OTHER BOOKS BY
CYNDI HARPER-DEITERS

JONATHAN MICHAEL THE RESIDENT ROOSTER
(verbal warning concept)
JONATHAN MICHAEL AND THE UNINVITED GUEST
(advisory problem-solving)
JONATHAN MICHAEL AND MOTHER NATURE'S FURY
(application of knowledge/frustration tolerance)
JONATHAN MICHAEL AND THE PERILOUS FLIGHT
(teamwork problem-solving)
JONATHAN MICHAEL AND THE PICKED POCKET
(nonviolent conflict resolution methods)
JONATHAN MICHAEL AND THE TWISTED TALE
(creative problem-solving, {preparation, incubation, inspiration, and verification})
JONATHAN MICHAEL AND THE FOREST FLOOR PROMISE
(goal directed thinking)
JONATHAN MICHAEL AND THE LANGUAGE TRAP
(trial and error)

ALL
PICTURE STORY BOOKS FOR:
AGES PRE-SCHOOL THROUGH THIRD

RIVER TURTLE
BOOK ONE OF THE
CLARA BROWNING SERIES

Chapter One...............Clara Denied..............Page.................1

Chapter Two..............Matthew's Rage...............Page.................7

Chapter Three...............Sheriff's Dilemma............Page.................11

Chapter Four..............Mrs. Miller's Packages.....Page.................13

Chapter Five..............The Red Dress.................Page.................15

Chapter Six..............Trapped.....................Page.................19

Chapter Seven..............The Mysterious Blemish...Page.................27

Chapter Eight..............Matthew's Convictions.....Page.................35

Chapter Nine.............."Girls Aren't Allowed".....Page.................39

Chapter Ten..............The Dreaded Job.............Page.................43

Chapter Eleven..............Dangerous Lesson #1.......Page.................49

Chapter Twelve..............Hazardous Thoughts.........Page.................53

Chapter Thirteen..........Branded Attraction...........Page.................59

Chapter Fourteen..........The Breeches.................Page.................75

Chapter Fifteen..............The Bank Robbery............Page.................85

Chapter Sixteen............A Voice In The Crowd.....Page.................93

Chapter Seventeen.........."Matthew Miller!"..........Page.................97

Chapter Eighteen..........Final Preparations...........Page.................101

Chapter Nineteen.........."On Your Mark!"...........Page.................105

Chapter Twenty............River Stranger.................Page.................109

Chapter Twenty-one.......The Deadly Crossing........Page.................113

Chapter Twenty-two........Making Up Lost Time......Page.................119

Chapter Twenty-three......Face to Face.....................Page.................125

Chapter Twenty-four.......The Murder.....................Page.................137

Chapter Twenty-five........Steeple Chase.................Page.................141

Chapter Twenty-six.........Naked Discovery.............Page.................149

Chapter Twenty-seven......Wasps.............................Page.................158

Chapter Twenty-eight.......Life or Death.................Page.................164

Chapter Twenty-nine........Surprised Emotions.........Page.................171

Chapter Thirty..............Captured.....................Page.................177

Chapter Thirty-one.........The Hide-Out.................Page.................181

Chapter Thirty-two.........Simon's Message............Page.................185

Chapter Thirty-three........The Rescue.....................Page.................187

Chapter Thirty-four.........The Finish Line..............Page.................198

Dedication:

**To all the Claras that have been, who are,
and that shall be.
Thank you for your strength and
determination that has, that is, and that
will cause waves of harmony through
understanding.**

Chapter 1
Clara Denied

Clara took her time getting ready for school. She hoped to speak with her father alone after her younger brother, Jake, left. She brushed her long hair and gathered it at the back of her neck, twisting it into a braid. That's the way her mother used to fix her hair. It made her feel close to her mother when she re-enacted things that she used to do. It had been so hard at first going on without her, but the older she got the more she felt her mother's presence.

"I wish these stupid freckles would disappear," she hissed into the mirror, wrinkling her small nose. Her father tried to tell her that the spirits touched her in the same way they had touched Flash. She knew he said that to try to make her feel better.

She slipped into her powder-blue dress with the crocheted collar that flattered her speckled face. "I hate wearing fancy dresses! Only sissies wear these ridiculous things! I can't even run fast in them! Whoever said girls should wear dresses obviously never wore one," she muttered to herself, the whole time pulling, snapping, and buttoning.

Finally she heard Jake slam the door behind him. She left her room and entered the kitchen. With its moist steam hanging like a dawn mist, the coffee's bitter aroma mingled with the fresh morning air. Her father stopped pouring his coffee when he noticed her.

"I see you're wearing the dress that reminds me of your mother," he said, looking up at her.

Clara had hoped he would notice. She thought that it might soften his mood when she asked again about Flash.

She walked slowly across the kitchen and put a thick, brown hotcake on her plate. The maple syrup was sticky and sweet as she poured it on her food and tasted it with the tip of her finger. She sat up straight in her chair to impress her father with her size.

"Father," she said quietly, "I've decided what I'd like for my birthday."

"Great! I've been hoping you'd let me know soon. Do I need to order it from Boston, San Francisco, or can I buy it from El Paso's finest general store, Bourbon's?" he asked, smiling across the table at her.

"Oh, no! I'm making it easy on you this year, Father. You just need to give me five dollars," she answered.

"Really, Clara? Have you finally come to value money? If you're going to take it to the bank, you should reconsider. I heard the Brewster Brothers are in the area. They may sneak right past me and rob the bank," he teased.

"No, I didn't plan to put it in the bank. I know a better way to make a lot of money with it," she said, looking down at her plate.

"Oh! Now I'm starting to understand," he said, pushing away from the table causing it to rock as he jumped to his feet.

"But, Father, you are being very unreasonable about this!" she cried.

"Unreasonable? Not wanting my daughter in a potentially death defying horse race does not make me unreasonable! This race is no place for a seventeen-year-old girl! In fact, it's no place for any female, regardless of her age!" he yelled.

"You see! That's the problem! You think females can't do a lot of things. My mother traveled here alone all the way from Chicago to be with you, and she survived, didn't she?" Clara stated firmly.

"That was another time and another place. That has nothing to do with you and that race," he said, not revealing the truth of her mother's adventure traveling here.

"It has everything to do with it! I inherited my mother's will! Even you said so! I can do anything I put my mind to, and my mind is made up! I'm entering and riding Flash in the race! I will win the race and use the money to go to veterinary school!" she yelled, jumping to her feet and knocking her chair over.

"You will not ride in that race, and you will not go to veterinary school! Neither is a proper place for a girl! Clara, you are a girl whether you like it or not! I am your father, and I aim to make you accept your proper role in life! If you want Flash to run the race, Pete will ride him! Not you!" he shouted, stomping out the door.

3

Clara picked up her chair and fell back into it. "I knew he wasn't going to agree to it, but I had to try," she cried. She didn't want to get into a big fight with him about it, but every time she had talked to him about going to school to be a veterinarian, he reacted like this. He didn't understand how desperately she wanted this. She had tried to get his approval, but he refused to listen to her. Left with no other choice, she began scheming to get into the race and the veterinary school.

Clara heard the pounding feet of the horses as the morning stage coach raced toward town. The stage still came often, even though, the Southern Pacific Railroad came almost two years earlier. It saddened her that her mother had not lived to celebrate the train's arrival on that warm May 13th day in 1881. In the past, not many people had traveled to El Paso. The wild flowing Río Grande on the west side and the rugged blue-shadowed Hueco Mountains along the north and east borders made passageways difficult. But with the train, many newcomers had shown up on the dusty streets of El Paso increasing its population almost daily.

She wished her mother were alive and celebrating her birthday with her. *"Mother would have been able to persuade father to let me ride Flash in the most popular race in Western Texas,"* she thought. Clara had dreamed often about running in the Mt. Franklin Race. Flash and she had always won the race in her dreams, and she knew dreams could come true if you believed in them.

She thought back to the first day she had laid her misty hazel eyes on Flash. On Clara's fourteenth

4

birthday, their mare, Lady, had given birth to a flawless white colt. It had only taken a few minutes for the colt to stand on his feet and run. Clara knew then he was going to be a great horse.

Clara put her black wool shawl over her thin shoulders as she left for school. Flash raced wildly through the tall prairie grass that grabbed at his hooves. He stopped running and snorted and whinnied at her. He lifted his two front legs and thrashed them harmoniously outward from his powerful body. His huge muscles bulging from his hindquarters bragged of his great strength and speed.

Clara rushed toward him to return his greeting. She leaned over the corral fencing and threw her arms around his thick neck. She buried her face in his neck and rubbed it with her small half-moon shaped chin. He responded by resting his massive head on her shoulder and nipping at the ends of her rusty red hair. She stepped back and told him how magnificent he was.

His snow-capped white hair shone like ice crystals reflecting the morning sun's rays. His matching, flowing mane, draped softly over his broad neck and covered his mysterious beauty mark. Father had said the beauty mark represented a blessing of the spirits. He said that the spirits had reached down from the mountaintops and touched Flash the day he was born. The mark of courage and greatness made Flash carry his head erectly and proudly.

She knew even though he was big and fast, he still needed much work to get him ready for the race. "You can win the race," she stated, unaware of Matthew Miller's intentions of keeping her from running in the race.

Chapter 2
Matthew's Rage

Matthew Miller saw her moving along the street in a dream-like state. He hated Clara because of her father. When Matthew was twelve years old, Sheriff Browning had shot and killed Matthew's father. Everyone, including his mother, said that the sheriff didn't have a choice, but that didn't matter to Matthew. All he knew was one day his father was there and the next day he wasn't.

He remembered when he was young how he had helped his father on their ranch. Sometimes, on a lazy Sunday afternoon, they had walked to the creek and went fishing together. When he got older, though, his father had changed. He had taken to drinking whiskey every day. When drunk, he beat Matthew often. Matthew had done most of the chores everyday then, because his father slept in mornings late and was too drunk in the evening to do them. He once had forced Matthew to sleep out in the barn, because Matthew had stepped between his mother and father when they were arguing.

It didn't matter, though, how bad his father had been. Matthew had known how good he could be. If the sheriff hadn't killed him, his father would be alive today and back to his normal self. He had promised to give up the drinking before he died, and Matthew believed he would. Because of that murdering sheriff, his father didn't have a chance to right his wrongs, which meant he was surely burning in hell forever!

Matthew had stopped going to school after his father's death. This had given him more time to take care of the animals and crops. Ranching took up all the daylight hours, so school and being with the other children of El Paso had been sacrificed. Today he had some fences to mend, so he came into town to get the fencing and nails he needed.

Clara passed Matthew without noticing him. She passed close enough to him that her dress brushed against his boots. "She's probably thinking about the race," Matthew muttered to himself. The thought of her horse in the race made him angry. He needed to win the race's purse before the County Commissioners took the ranch for unpaid taxes. He had tried his best to make ends meet, but the droughts the past two years had left them penniless. His mother's seamstress shop barely made enough money to pay for itself. He had never said anything to her about it, though. He knew how much she loved sewing and being in town with people everyday.

It had been six years since his father's death. Matthew had often wondered why his mother didn't remarry. After all, she was a very handsome woman. She always wore small dried flowers around the tight bun she spun in her ash blond hair. Her small bones fit nicely under her pale skin. Her figure almost matched that of the saloon girls that were always dancing and twirling about. Matthew knew that it couldn't be the memory of his father. He had stopped trying to figure it out, though, because one thing he had learned from his father was, women are too hard to understand.

As he watched Clara walk into the school, he turned toward Bourbon's unaware of the budding relationship between his mother and the sheriff he hated so deeply.

Chapter 3
Sheriff's Dilemma

"That girl is going to have to settle down soon and learn to cook, sew, and care for a home and family," Sheriff Browning told his deputy while pacing the jail's floor.

"Maybe you need to send her off to spend some time with some women, so she can learn," Deputy Quill answered.

"Maybe you're right. I have to get that fool notion out of her head that she's going to ride in the Mt. Franklin Race. I sure wish her ma were here to get her under control," he said.

Deputy Quill smiled and thought to himself, *"It's because of Clara's ma's blood that she is so darned stubborn now. If her ma were alive, she'd be helping her train that foolish horse so she could ride him in the race herself."*

"Maybe she could spend some time at Mrs. Miller's shop after school each day helping her out. At the same time, she could be learning some sewing," Sheriff Browning said.

"Now there's a good idea, Sheriff," Deputy Quill replied.

"I'll talk to Clara about it tonight, and see what she thinks of the idea."

"Why ask her? You know she's not going to fancy the idea!"

"You have a good point. Maybe I'll speak with Mrs. Miller first and see if she'd be interested. I'll offer to pay her something. I'll stop around her shop later today. But for now, I must get over to the bank to accompany Lawrence to the train station," he said, not realizing the accidental meeting that was going to occur at the train station.

Chapter 4
Mrs. Miller's Packages

"If that material is not on the train today, I don't know how I'm going to get all this sewing for Mrs. Wilkinson finished in time for the party," Mrs. Miller sputtered to Bezzie, her plump yellow cat curled up in the window seat soaking up the lukewarm spring sun. "I'll be heading over to the train station to check on that material order. You mind the shop while I'm gone, Bezzie," Mrs. Miller said, taking off her crisp white cotton apron and smoothing down her pale blond hair.

Sheriff Browning and the banker reached the train station platform at the same time Mrs. Miller did. The train huffed and heaved and coughed up its congestion.

The conductor helped passengers off and tried to direct the unloading of the train's cargo at the same time. When he saw Mrs. Miller heading toward the station door, he called out to her, "Mrs. Miller, I have that order of yours. I loaded it myself day before yesterday."

"That's splendid! I've been just frantic about that order since it missed last week's train. Tell me where I can find it," she answered loudly, so he could hear her over the noise.

"It's being unloaded now. I'll bring it to the shop for you. It's rather heavy," the conductor replied.

"Oh, that's quite all right!" Sheriff Browning yelled, approaching Mrs. Miller. "I had planned to stop over at your shop today anyway, so I'll bring the packages to you."

Mrs. Miller smiled and said, "Thank you, Sheriff. I'll be going back to the shop now. I'm sure Bezzie has drifted off to sleep and isn't watching it well."

Sheriff Browning and the banker, Lawrence, watched until the local mine's payroll was taken out of the safe in the railroad president's car. "I don't know why you take such a risk holding that money in your bank. The mine's foreman could come and get it from the train just as easily as from your bank, Lawrence," Sheriff Browning said.

"Well, Sheriff, they make it well worth my while. Besides, I ain't had a lick of trouble all these years with it. Next month they'll be bringing in an extra five thousand dollars for the race's purse. I'll be holding that for close to a month before the race. Heck, Sheriff, I'm not worried as long as you're in town," he replied.

"Come on. Let's not stand around here looking for trouble with all this money," Sheriff Browning said, picking up Mrs. Miller's packages with his free hand.

The sheriff walked Lawrence back to the bank and waited until he had counted and locked the money in the bank's safe. He left the bank and headed down the street toward Mrs. Miller's shop. Whistling a favorite tune, he noticed that the trees and bushes in the foothills had turned green. "Guess it's a sure-fire sign that spring is here," he mumbled, walking toward an unexpected encounter.

Chapter 5
The Red Dress

Mrs. Miller busily pressed a dress she had just finished for Betsy from the saloon. She really hated making those saloon girls' dresses, because she didn't approve of their style of living, but it was money to help pay the bills. She did it despite her feelings.

"I must admit, it sure is a pretty thing. I wonder what I'd look like in that bright red material. The ruffles must tickle when brushing up against one's bare chest," she teased Bezzie, who was paying no attention to her at the time.

She didn't know what came over her, but she instantly dropped her dress down around her ankles and slipped Betsy's dress over her head. She just finished snapping up the dress's back when Sheriff Browning walked in. Embarrassed, her face turned just as red as the dress. Stammering, she looked around for a shawl or a piece of material to put over herself, but in her frustrated frame of mind she could see nothing within reach to use. The ruffle tickled her bare flesh as she straightened up and looked at the at the Sheriff. Trying to compose herself, she said with dignity in her voice, "Thank you, Sheriff Browning, for bringing my parcels over. I truly appreciate it."

"It's my pleasure, Ma'am," he replied, trying to keep his eyes on her face.

"Well, I'll not keep you," she said, hoping he would leave.

"I had hoped to speak with you about my daughter, Clara," he said.

"Your daughter? What about Clara?" she asked.

"Seems she's getting close to being a full-grown woman sooner than I expected. Her growing up without a ma and all has left her unprepared for those things women need to know about. I had hoped you could help me out," he replied.

"Dear me, do you mean she needs a talking about, well--about the birds and bees?" she asked in a whisper, leaning toward him, so he could hear.

Now it was his turn for embarrassment. "No! Not that at all! I'm talking about cooking and sewing and the like," he answered, looking down at his hat that had been in his hand since entering the shop.

"Oh, I see. How can I be of help, Sheriff?" she asked politely.

"I thought perhaps she could come and help you in your shop afternoons. She could learn sewing from you and proper woman behavior. I'd gladly pay you for your trouble," he answered.

"I'm sure an arrangement can be made. I'm working on a big project now. It would help to have someone like Clara to work with me," she said.

"But, I'm not sure how much help she will be, Mrs. Miller. She doesn't know a thing about sewing. Matter of fact, she hates the idea of doing any kind of woman chores. I haven't even mentioned this arrangement to her, because I'm sort of afraid of her reaction. She can be downright stubborn if she has a mind to. I'll discuss it with her tonight. If she agrees, I'll send her over Monday after school," he said, looking into her ribbon-blue eyes.

"Very well, Sheriff, you stop by and let me know what the decision is. But if you don't mind me saying so, I'd say that maybe what she needs is a switching if she can't accept her responsibilities without making a fuss."

"You have a darned good point, Mrs. Miller, but I'm afraid a switching wouldn't change that girl's mind once it's made up. She takes after her mother, God rest her soul."

"I'll look forward to her coming, if that is what's decided," she said, moving toward the door, hoping he would take the gesture as a polite prod to leave.

"Afternoon, Ma'am," he said putting his hat on and turning for the door. Before he left though, he turned back just one more time to see Mrs. Miller in that beautiful red dress. My, she was a beauty in it. He had never noticed what a beautiful woman she was before. "Might I say, Mrs. Miller, that dress looks mighty fine on you?"

"Why, thank you, Sheriff, but I was just checking the fit. It's not my style, as I'm sure you know," she stammered, wishing he would leave.

The bell rang on the door as he shut it behind him. She dropped back on the window seat, exhausted from the emotional strain of embarrassment, not to mention the giggles she had been stifling from the ruffles brushing up against her chest. "Oh, dear me! What in the world had possessed me to put this flimsy dress on in the first place?" she asked herself as she pulled open the snaps.

Sheriff Browning walked slowly toward the jail. *"My! My! She sure is one beautiful woman! Wonder how come I never paid her much mind before? If Clara agrees to go there, I'll be able to admire her more often,"* he thought. Slowly, he began whistling, but this time it was a new tune; one he had not whistled in a very long time. It brought back memories of Clara as a young child. He couldn't know this very night she would be defending herself with an unusual weapon.

Chapter 6
Trapped

Clara left the school in a hurry. Eager to get home and change into something less ladylike, she pushed ahead of the other students.

Entering the house, she picked up an apple and went into her room. She pulled the dress over her head and hung it on its peg. She grabbed her pants and pulled them on and tucked her cotton shirt inside before fastening them. Holding the apple in her mouth, she pulled her boots on and then her jacket.

She stopped at the door and put on her hat. "Now, I feel like me!" she spouted like an overheated teakettle.

Flash saw her coming and greeted her in his normal way. He lifted his front legs off the ground and extended them before him. She ran quickly to the gate. Taking one last bite of the sour apple, she held it out for Flash to take from her. "Come on, Flash, we have work to do before Father gets home," she said, pulling him toward the barn. Once inside, she put his bridle and saddle on him. "Today we are going to practice pacing at a steady gait," she told him, rubbing his nose. He whinnied in response to her gentle touch.

She led him outside and mounted him with grace and ease, just as she had been doing the past year. She turned him toward the jagged mountains and gave him a gentle nudge. He ran against the wind, racing its invisible force. She let him run at his will over the small mounds of desert earth that rolled from one small heap to the next until she was out of sight of the house. She pulled back on the reins and said, "Whoa!" He stopped, as asked. She nudged him gently, but firmly, in the side and again he began running at a tremendous speed. She pulled on the worn leather reins gently to slow him, but he stopped. "That's the problem with you, Flash, you only know two speeds, fast and stop! You need to learn to walk and trot. We can't win the race just because you run fast. You'll tire quickly and we won't make the first ten miles of the race," she stated loudly.

She gently nudged him again, and off he went, running as if he were fleeing danger. "No, Flash, don't run!" she yelled, pulling back on the reins. Again, he stopped. "No, Flash, don't stop!" she cried angrily. "Look! When I nudge you slightly that means walk. If I put more pressure in the nudge, I want you to gallop. If I press my heels in deep, that means run. Do you understand?" she asked.

Flash snorted and raised his head up and down following the steady beat of his heart, as if to say, "Yes, I understand."

She nudged him gently. He ran! She pulled back on the reins with a slight amount of pressure to slow him. He stopped! This went on for hours until she could see orange rays of the setting sun streaking across the western sky.

While she worked with Flash, José watched the horse and rider wrestle with each other. Groans of disappointment mingled with the crushing of rocks under the enormous animal. José had become a faithful spectator of these training sessions over the past few weeks. It didn't appear to him, though, that she had made any progress. She didn't know he had watched, because he did so while working on Mr. Wilkinson's nearby ranch. He pulled his sombrero tighter over his head to block the sun's blazing evening rays.

Clara turned Flash toward home. She slouched in the saddle feeling disappointed. He still didn't understand anything but run and stop. She wouldn't give up, though. She knew he was smart and eventually he would learn. She just hoped it was in time for the race.

She gave him some hay after cooling him down. She cleaned his tattered leather tack with special oiled soap while he ate. It was getting dark. She figured she ought to get into the house to set the table for supper. As she started to open the door, she saw a shadow about her size move across the light from the lantern she held. She picked up a pitch fork. Holding it above her head as a weapon, she opened the door demanding, "Who's there?"

"Don't be afraid señorita. My name is José."

"What are you doing sneaking around here? What do you want?" she asked crossly.

"The horse, señorita," he answered.

"He isn't for sale. Now, you get out of here before I scream."

"No, señorita, I didn't figure he was for sale. I wanted to talk to you about his training."

"What training?" she asked him, lowering the pitch fork.

"The training you have been doing," he answered.

"What do you know about that?" she asked.

"I know he only does two things: run and stop. And, I figured that you were trying to teach him more."

"That's true, but what does it have to do with you coming here tonight?" she asked.

"I wanted to offer my services, señorita," he answered with a big smile.

"What services are those, José?" she asked, interested.

"I have watched my papá and abuelo (grandfather) train many horses. I believe that I can help you with your horse. What do you call him?" he asked.

"His name is Flash. I don't have any money to pay a trainer, so you best be on your way," she said, walking toward him.

"I don't ask for money, señorita. I offer to help you free of money."

"Why would you offer to do that?" she asked.

"Because, I know you and your Flash need the help and I need the practice," he answered.

"So, if I let you help me, what's in it for you?" she asked.

"I ask that once he is trained you let my father see what a good job I do with your horse. Then he will believe it is time for me to begin training Mr. Wilkinson's fine horses," he answered.

"Well, the best that I can do, José, is promise you I'll think about it," she said, walking toward the barn door.

"Fine, señorita, you think about it. I'll see you next time you take Flash out for training," he said, slipping out the barn door ahead of her.

Reaching the house, she smelled beef frying. "Oh, dear. Father beat me home again," she thought. She stopped at the well for a bucket of water. She pushed the door open and spilled water all over the kitchen floor when the door bounced off the bucket.

"So! Clara, you came home!" Sheriff Browning said, turning from the stove.

"Sorry, Father, I lost track of the time."

"Well, now that you found the time please set the table. Supper is almost ready."

She couldn't believe it. Wasn't he going to give her that responsibility speech that she had heard almost every night the past few weeks?

Just as she had finished setting the table, her little brother, Jake, came stumbling through the door with an armful of wood. Sheriff Browning put the food on the table. They began to eat. Jake got a crooked grin on his face and said, "Father, I know where Clara has been tonight. Shall I tell you?"

"Don't bother, you little snitch! I'll tell him where I was! It's none of your business, you little spy!" she yelled at him.

"Now, you two settle down. Very well, Clara, where were you?" he asked, while putting potatoes on his plate.

"I was out with Flash," she said.

"You liar, Clara! I saw you talking to some boy out at the barn!" Jake cried.

"Is this true, Clara?" Father asked.

"Yes, I guess so. Although, I didn't invite him here," she answered.

"So, who was he, and what did he want?" Sheriff Browning asked.

"He said his name was José, and he was looking for work," she lied, but it was only a half lie.

"And, what did you tell him?" the sheriff asked.

"I told him we didn't need help," she answered.

"You're right, Clara, we don't need a hired hand other than Pete. We seem to manage our chores well. That's why I have this surprise for you," he said.

It wasn't often Father offered something, so Clara became quite interested in what he had to say.

"Really, Father, a surprise for me? What is it?" she asked excitedly.

"A job in town after school. It pays little," he answered, hoping he was playing his cards right. He had to be sneaky with Clara and get her really interested before telling her the whole thing.

Chewing her meat, she thought how she could use money to buy supplies for the race. "How much would it pay, Father?" she asked.

"About a dollar a week, I think," he answered.

She figured in her head it would be seven or eight dollars in earnings before the race.

"What kind of work is it, Father?" she inquired.

"A type you've never done before, but I know you are interested in learning new things, right?"

She nodded her head in agreement to his question. He felt pleased. He had hooked her. Now slowly he began to reel her in.

"She needs you after school each day and some on Saturday for now. I think you would find it good mind-stimulating work," he said.

"Sounds perfect! When do I start?" she asked.

"Does Monday suit you?" he asked, pleased with his successful trickery.

"That would be just fine, Father. Now, do tell me where am I to go Monday after school?" she asked anxiously.

"To Mrs. Miller's shop," he replied.

She wasn't thrilled with the prospect of working in a seamstress shop, but she had committed herself. She really could use the money. Besides, maybe she could learn, while working there, how to make a pair of pants that would fit her more comfortably for the long race.

"Very well. Mrs. Miller's it is!" she said, working up a smile so her father would feel proud of himself for cleverly tricking her. She knew all along what he was up to. Most times she wouldn't let him get away with it. Sometimes she had to make him feel good, and this time she did, because she wanted the money. This same money would buy her more trouble and danger than she ever dreamt possible.

Chapter 7
The Mysterious Blemish

The next morning, Clara hurried about the house with her indoor weekend chores: shaking rugs, sweeping floors, and dusting furniture. As soon as she finished, she rushed out to the barn where Flash waited. She gave him some oats while she gently brushed his flawless white body. There was not a single hair on his body that wasn't pure white, except his birthmark. She lifted his long, silky mane and brushed along his glossy neck. Putting the brush down, she traced the mark with the tip of her finger. The marking had a familiar shape, one she had seen before, but could never recall from where. She pushed all thoughts from her mind and focused on the mark. "Think! Think, Clara! Where have you seen this shape before?" she demanded of herself. She squeezed her eyes tightly shut, until she could see white speckles. Darkened lines with outlines of white mixed with gray entered her view. "Concentrate! Where is the shape from?" she asked the darkness of her inner self. Like so many times before, the answer didn't come.

"Oh! What does it matter anyway?" she sputtered, dropping Flash's mane against his neck.

She gathered up his tack and began to put his saddle on. "Flash, are you going to pay attention to me today?" she asked him, tightening the girth around his stomach. He turned his head and nudged her with his nose as she brought the cinch around the second time into a tight knot. "I'm going to assume that means yes," she said, smiling at him over her shoulder. She saw her reflection in his deep brown eyes as she put on his bridle. "Nasty freckles!" she spat at her image.

She led him out of the barn. She slid up into the saddle and gave him a gentle nudge. Off with the speed of a lynx, he ran with long strides. His hooves landed like thunderbolts on the dry, hardened earth. Each landing added an untamed bounce to his heated gait. Clara held on with all the strength her arms could muster. Her hat flew off and tumbled in the wild swirls of the wind that Flash's speed made. Hair flew all around her face and the ends gathered to make a whip-cracking sound with each pounding footfall. His mane flew back against her chest and tickled her in her nose, causing her to sneeze. Tears formed in her eyes from the wind slapping into them. She squinted them out and new ones formed and fell silently behind the others. She allowed him to run like a scared antelope. She hoped to tire him a bit before the training began. However, she had no idea hat Flash could run like this for miles without experiencing exhaustion.

She tightened her grip on the reins and pulled up and back at the same time. She pulled herself straight up in the saddle and gave the command "Whoa!" Flash did as asked of him and stopped. His nostrils flared wide from catching the wind directly in them. He pawed the ground as if to say he needed more freedom to run. "Good boy, Flash," Clara said, patting his neck. She looked around to see if José was anywhere in sight. "Good! I don't have any spies today," she stated firmly.

"Okay, Flash here we go. I want you to walk. That does not mean run. I'm going to gently nudge you. You will walk slowly," Clara said, moving herself slowly in the saddle. She gently nudged him with the heel of her boot, but Flash did not walk as she had told him. He immediately leaped forward with great force, almost throwing her out of the saddle, and began to run again. She pulled back on the reins and yelled, "Whoa!" He stopped instantly.

"Flash, what is wrong with you?" she asked him crossly. "How many times do I have to explain this to you?" Again she nudged. Again he ran.

José had watched Clara's and Flash's ritual for almost an hour. The pattern had not changed. She nudged. He ran. She pulled back. He stopped. There was nothing in between. José knew he could train Flash. If he could prove to his father that he was ready for horse training, he could quit working as the ranch's stable boy.

José had often thought of how great it would be to train wild horses like his father and grandfather. Seeing himself as a great horseman, José walked across the plowed field and turned toward the base of the mountain where Clara and Flash were. Clara saw him out of the corner of her eye and pretended she didn't. "The last thing I need is some boy telling me how to teach you a few simple things!" she snorted.

"Señorita, how are you this fine morning?" José asked.

29

"I'm quite fine, thank you, José," she answered politely.

"I've been watching you and your horse, Flash. He still does not want to change his ways, does he señorita?" José said, smiling so widely it almost matched the width of his sombrero brim.

"It'll take some time, but I'm sure I can teach him to do what I ask," Clara said, without returning his smile.

José walked up to Flash and firmly clamped his hand around the reins close to the bit. "You, Flash, are a fury, are you not?" he asked. José slowly turned Flash around in a small circle. "Do you see your legs, Flash?" he asked. Then he turned him slowly in another tight circle in the opposite direction. "Now, Flash, can you also see your legs from this direction?" José asked the horse. "Legs give you power, Flash. They can take you many places in many speeds. Your legs, they either do not take Flash, or they take Flash fast. These legs can walk and trot, too, but only if you let them. The next time you are running instead of walking like Clara wants you to, she only need pull you into a tight circle so you can see your legs. Then, Flash, measure your legs' speed with the pressure of the bit in your mouth and see if they match. If not, you'll need to adjust the speed of your legs, because they are the only things you have control over."

José then released the horse's reins. He turned toward Clara. Taking off his sombrero and bowing briefly, he bid her good day. Turning to leave, he shifted his head sideways to catch a glance at horse and rider. He then continued past the field toward the ranch.

"Well, pardon me for not applauding such a great man!" Clara sneered in José's direction. "Come on, Flash, we have work to do. Now, you better just pay attention this time and do as I ask you. I'm beginning to lose my patience with you," she said, as she turned him back toward the mountains.

"Remember. A gentle nudge means walk," she reminded the horse, and gently nudged him. Again, he leaped forward and positioned himself for the race against the wind. Caught off balance, Clara fell to the ground smashing her knees into the iron hard earth. Material stretched as fibers were forced apart from the intensity of the fall. She felt blood trickle out the hole in her pant leg. The cut stung as she picked the pieces of dirt and small stones out of it. "Gol-darnit, Flash! Can't you understand anything?" she yelled after him, picking herself up and brushing off.

Flash turned and came back toward her, as if he knew she was missing from the saddle. Clara reached up and slid her hand down his face and rubbed his nose. "Oh, it's too hard to stay mad at you, Flash," Clara said, pulling the canteen from the saddle. She lifted it high and took a deep drink and let the cool water run down her hot, swollen throat. Then she cupped her bruised hand and poured some in and let Flash lick it up.

Clara fastened the canteen back to the saddle and lifted herself into it. "Now, easy boy; let's try this again," she said, gripping the reins and reinforcing her leg-hold. She wasn't taking any chances of falling off again as she steadied herself and prepared for the take-off. She gently nudged and he ran. She began thinking about what José had said. "Look at your legs, Flash, do they measure the pressure of the bit?" she asked him, pulling the left rein out and forcing his neck to turn in toward his body. Suddenly, he was going in a circle and his speed had broken to a slow trot. She released the pulling of the left rein and slowly moved it back toward his front legs. He came out of the circle and began running again. Again, she pulled the left rein out and forced his neck tight to his body until he was trotting in a circle. "You see, Flash, the measure is equal between the speed of your legs and that of the bit's pressure," she said, feeling triumph. All that afternoon she made him check his measure when he would run off with her. He eventually acted as if he understood that the meaning of the circles was to slow him. Clara decided he had come a long way this day, but he had much farther to go before the race. She hadn't noticed José watching.

José felt triumph, too. He felt pleased that Clara understood what he had told Flash about checking his measure of speed. They swirled dust and sand all around them the entire afternoon, practicing. José could already see that Flash was easing up on the speed after hours of circles. "It has just begun, Flash," he said in their direction.

Clara took Flash back to the barn and replaced his tack with a heavy gray wool blanket. "You stay here and rest. I'll be back in a while to brush and feed you. Right now I have to hang the

32

clothes that have been soaking most of the day, before Father gets home and I get into trouble," Clara said, walking out the barn door. At the same time, Matthew, ten miles away, walked an exhausted team toward home thinking of Clara.

Chapter 8
Matthew's Convictions

Matthew walked the team slowly toward the barn. He didn't feel like rushing them home after a long day of fencing. He felt physically drained like a wrung out rag from the two days he had just spent out in the pasture. "Thank God all that fencing is behind us, boys," he said, as a big yawn escaped him. He knew he had many chores waiting for him, so he slightly lifted and released the reins, so the horses would pick up their pace just a little. As they trotted, Clara's face came into his mind. "I know Raven can outrun that little pony of hers any day of the week," he sputtered into the cool air.

Once inside the barn, Matthew unhitched the wagon. He took the heavy yokes off the huge work horses and slipped the leather harnesses and reins from them. He opened the barn door and the horses rushed by him.

With tired, heavy legs he climbed up the wooden ladder one rung at a time to the hay mound and pitched several forks of hay out into the corral. Matthew felt glad that spring was coming. The horses would need to start pasturing soon as the hay supply was getting very low. Matthew jumped down and went for water buckets for the cows. After tying the two cows up, he gave them their water. He firmly gripped two swollen cow teats and pulled down firmly as warm milk flowed and fell into the metal bucket causing a swishing sound as it bounced into its empty bottom. Matthew didn't think much about milking, but only of those things that he had to do before nightfall.

Mrs. Miller greeted Matthew at the door when he brought in a bucket of milk and a bucket of water. "Why, Matthew, you look exhausted," she cooed, touching his shoulder.

"Yeah, Ma, guess you're right there. I have a few more chores to do before supper. I'm sure hoping you got some of that good cooking of yours ready, because I'm powerful hungry," Matthew said, turning to leave the long wooden porch.

"Don't you fret, Son, I've got lots of food for you," she said, smiling. "Poor Matthew. He works so hard around here taking care of this ranch and us," Mrs. Miller said to Bezzie.

Matthew finished the chores. Outside by the well, he washed his dry, cracked hands. His fingers ended in broken dirt packed nails. One fingernail was bruised black under its surface because he had accidentally hit it instead of the fence post. When he opened the door the smell of fresh-baked bread greeted him.

"Have a seat, Son. Supper is ready," his mother said, setting a heaping dish of potatoes and carrots on the table.

Matthew smeared freshly churned butter on the warm bread. With butter dripping off the edges and onto his plate, he fit a large piece in his mouth. "This here food is a sight better than that I fixed myself out in the pasture," he said with a mouthful.

"I'm sure sorry, Matthew, that you have to work so hard, and by yourself, too," his ma answered.

"Oh, never you mind, Ma. I'm doing just fine. Things are working fine around here. The animals are all healthy, spring is just around the corner, and I have a feeling it's going to be a great crop year."

"Matthew, you don't have to pretend with me. I know that our back taxes are near due and we don't have the money. I just don't see how we are going to be able to hold on to this ranch much longer," she said quietly.

"Ma, don't you be fretting about it. I have it all worked out. I'm going to take care of you and the ranch, so you just take care of your sewing shop and let me take care of the rest."

"But, Matthew, how are you going to come up with that kind of money this year? We haven't paid a dime the past few years. This year after harvest we will owe two years worth of payments at the bank and three years' back taxes," she replied.

"Ma, you know how fast and powerful Raven is, don't you?" Matthew asked between bites of food.

"Yes, I know how well Raven can run," his Ma answered.

"Well, I'm fixing to enter him into the Mt. Franklin Race. I know he can win the race. I've been through those canyons many times, Ma, and I know I can win. The race's purse is five thousand dollars. That would be enough to pay the bank off and the back taxes."

"Matthew, that race is dangerous! There are men from all around these parts that come to run that race. Some men have died trying to win that race. I'm not going to allow my only son to ride in it, ranch or no ranch!" Mrs. Miller exclaimed.

"Oh, Ma, see how you are? I'm not a little boy anymore. I'm as big as any man in El Paso. I aim to enter that race and win it, Ma, with or without your consent," he stated firmly, pushing his chair from the table.

"As much as I hate to admit it, you are a grown man. You prove that every day the way you run this place. I expect whether I want you to ride in that race or not, I'll not be stopping you, but I'll not be encouraging you either," she stated harshly, getting up and loudly banging and clearing dishes from the table.

"Ma, I don't mean to upset you, but a man has to do what he thinks is best. I'll be joining you for church tomorrow," he said, unprepared for the brief church confrontation with Clara that was coming.

Chapter 9
"Girls Aren't Allowed"

The sheriff and his two children entered church a little later than usual. The only seats left were toward the front by the Millers. Sheriff Browning led the way up the aisle and motioned for Clara to move into the pew first. She went in ahead of her father and brother and sat down next to Matthew. He shifted toward his mother a little more to give her some extra room.

Clara hadn't seen Matthew for some time. He didn't come to school anymore, so she didn't see him often. He didn't always come to church service with his mother, either. She wondered why he was at the service with her today. She tried not to stare at Matthew, but she couldn't help herself. He seemed to tower over her. His golden-rye hair barely touched his shoulders that were broader than her father's. His hands were as wide as the Bible he held. She lifted her eyes slowly to get a quick glimpse of his face. He caught her off guard when their eyes met. His eyes were just as blue as his mother's. She quickly looked down at her lap and began to roll the ribbon on her dress through her fingers.

When the service was over, she jumped up and pushed past her father and brother and bolted toward the door. She didn't want to take the chance of being caught looking at Matthew again. She went to their buggy and leaned against it looking toward the church doors. Her father and brother came out with the Millers. Mrs. Miller and Sheriff Browning were speaking to each other on the top step. She watched Matthew standing behind his mother. He looked angry, she thought. She couldn't believe how tall and big he was.

Clara knew Matthew saw her looking at him, but this time she did not turn her head away. Why should she? There was no crime in looking at people. It just wasn't polite, that's all. She watched as Matthew excused himself from his mother and walked down the church steps toward one of the foreman from the mine. The two of them walked over to a nearby wagon. She saw Matthew hand the foremen some money and then he gave Matthew a piece of paper. Matthew wrote on the paper and then gave it back to him. "Now I know why he came to service with his mother. He is entering his name in the race," she whispered to herself.

When Matthew walked past her, she called out to him, "Matthew, what horse are you riding in the race?" she asked him politely.

"Raven, of course. He's the fastest horse in the territory. I'm going to win this race, Clara. I've got the best darned horse to ride and I know all those canyons out there like my back yard. Ain't no sense in you entering your little Flash in the race. The trail through the mountains will kill him," Matthew answered smugly.

"Is that so, Matthew Miller!" she spat at him. "I think you better just keep one thing in mind! I'll be looking over my shoulder at you when I cross the finish line!"

40

"I don't have any fear that you'll be winning the race, Clara. Besides you ain't riding in the race anyway. Girls aren't allowed to run the Race. And the last time I knew, you were a girl," he said in a cocky tone.

"Well, girl or no girl, I'm going to show you who has the best horse for the race! You just wait and see! There ain't nothing you can do that I can't do better! So you best be worrying about who can and cannot ride in that race," Clara stated firmly.

Matthew walked away from her shaking his head and laughing. His behavior really made her angry. "Men! Just who do they think they are anyway? They tell me that I'm not good enough to join men in a race, but I'm good enough to make men's pants to wear in a saddle. I'll show that brat which of us wears the best riding pants in that race!" she muttered angrily.

Chapter 10
The Dreaded Job

Monday after school, Clara walked toward Mrs. Miller's seamstress shop. She didn't see José standing in front of Bourbon's until she walked into him. "Excuse me, señorita," he said, tipping his sombrero.

"José! I'm sorry. I wasn't paying attention to where I was going. I was busy thinking about how much better Flash did yesterday afternoon with his lessons," she said, feeling slightly embarrassed.

"Yes, I know that your Flash did better yesterday. But, señorita, he has a long way to go before the big race, no?"

"Yes, he does. But I know he'll be ready. He is a good horse," she said.

"Señorita, have you considered my services?" José asked.

"Well, I have thought about it some. It will be okay, I guess. But I don't want you taking over Flash. He is my horse. I know what is best for him. Also, I don't believe in hitting horses or doing anything mean to them to make them learn," she replied.

"No, no, señorita, I would never use force on a horse. I promise you that. When can we begin the training?" he asked.

"Tomorrow at five o'clock. I'll meet you out by the Wilkinson's fields," she answered, walking away.

The bell rang on the shop door when Clara stepped inside the small room. Mrs. Miller came out from the back to greet her caller. "Good afternoon, Clara. I trust you had a splendid day in school."

"Yes, I did, Mrs. Miller. My father told me you will be needing me about two hours a day. I hope he told you that I know nothing about sewing. And just so you know right up front, I don't particularly care for this type of thing. Needles and thread and sewing quilts and the such doesn't interest me much. But I will work hard and I promise that I will pay attention to those tasks you teach me," Clara announced carefully.

"Clara, I appreciate your honesty. Two hours a day it is. Shall we get started?" Mrs. Miller asked, motioning for Clara to follow her into the back room of the shop.

Clara was surprised with all the beautiful cotton, silk, and velvet materials that lay draped all over in the back room. She jumped when she saw a slight movement under a piece of pale pink material in the window seat. Then she laughed when a big fluffy, yellow cat stuck its head out from under the material and meowed.

"Oh, yes, Clara, do meet Bezzie. He is my faithful assistant," Mrs. Miller said, playfully reaching over to pick up Bezzie from his hiding place.

"He certainly is a fat cat!" Clara said, laughing at her own temporary fear.

"All he does is eat and sleep. Occasionally he attempts to catch a mouse. But most of the time

44

he prefers whatever I'm eating and he isn't shy about asking for some of it, either," she laughed, putting him down on the seat.

There were huge white cupboards and drawers built on the wall from the ceiling to the floor on the east side of the room. Mrs. Miller pulled open a large drawer and motioned for Clara to step closer to her. "This is where I keep all the thread. I have it organized in color groups. Starting with black and working back and forth alphabetically. I must insist that you keep the drawer organized, because it makes the job much easier," she said firmly.

Mrs. Miller continued opening drawers and cupboards showing Clara where the buttons, snaps, elastic, ribbons, lace, and needles were all kept. They were all organized just the way she described. Each time, Mrs. Miller reminded her that they were to remain that way. Mrs. Miller moved over to the northeast corner of the room and there stood a strange looking thing. "This is my favorite spot in the shop," Mrs. Miller said, sitting down behind the strange object.

"I do all my sewing in the morning right here, so I can soak up the sun," she said running her hand over the top of the black iron thing.

"Mrs. Miller, if you don't mind my asking, what is that thing?" Clara asked, staring at the contraption.

"Why, Clara, it is the latest model sewing machine. You didn't think we sewed everything by hand, did you?" Mrs. Miller asked.

"Yes, I did think that, Mrs. Miller. I've never heard of a machine doing the sewing," she answered, walking up to the sewing machine.

"No wonder you don't particularly like to sew. Heavens, it would take us a month of Sundays to get one small job done if we were doing it all by hand," Mrs. Miller laughed.

Mrs. Miller stood up and took Clara by the hand and sat her down behind the machine. She began explaining to her how the machine operated. "As the machine stitches the material it advances the material through for the next stitch. The material is held in tight by the pressure foot. The pedal to run the machine is right down there by your feet. Now, lift your feet and place them on the pedal. Slowly lift your feet up until you're on your toes and then slowly lower your feet down to a flat position and then repeat the motion all over again," Mrs. Miller encouraged Clara.

"This is fascinating!" Clara exclaimed, even though she wasn't sewing anything at the time.

"It is better than fascinating." Mrs. Miller agreed, "It is the best machine ever invented. I worked on others when I was a young girl training in San Antonio, but they were completely awkward compared to this one."

"Will I learn how to use this machine?" Clara asked, surprising herself.

"Eventually you will, Clara, but for now, we have to get at the work that must be done today," Mrs. Miller answered.

Mrs. Miller led the way to the front of the shop. The afternoon sun filled the room with a toasty warmth. Clara looked out the big window facing the street. She heard spurs dancing on men's boots as they passed by. Mrs. Miller placed a large bolt of bright daffodil yellow material on a long counter and began measuring it by holding the bolt against her chest and unrolling the material out as far as she could along the length of her arm. After three arm lengths, she marked it and laid it on the counter. She took the scissors and cut the material off the bolt.

"Now, Clara, I need you to pin this pattern onto the material. I'll show you exactly how to do it. Once it is pinned, you will then cut it out for me and pin the seams together."

Clara paid attention to Mrs. Miller's instructions, but not nearly as closely as she would to José's instructions given tomorrow under unpleasant circumstances.

Chapter 11
Dangerous Lesson #1

Tuesday afternoon José watched from Mr. Wilkinson's for Clara and Flash. He finished his work for the day and made excuses to his father about why he was unable to come home right away. The days were getting longer and warmer now. José enjoyed the spring's mild heat. Although he had grown accustomed to the hot summer sun, he preferred the moderate heat of the spring and fall.

Clara saw José as she reached the crest of the hill. He waved at her and sang out, "Good afternoon, señorita."

"Good afternoon, José," she replied, waving at him.

José walked up to Flash and put his hand out to catch the rein Clara was handing to him as she dismounted. "Is Flash ready to learn today?" José asked, rubbing Flash's nose.

"He better be, because the race will soon be here. "Well, José, what do we do now?" she asked him, smiling.

"Today we work on voice command, señorita. I will lunge Flash with you on his back," José answered, picking up a long rope from the ground.

José fastened the rope around Flash's head in a halter style. It fit over his nose and behind his ears. Flash danced a little when José tightened the rope on his nose. "Now, señorita, I will stand here.

You lead Flash out as far as you can until you come to the end of the rope."

Clara did as José said. She got to the end of the rope, stopped, and remounted. José stood about thirty feet from her tightly holding the other end of the rope.

"Señorita, nudge Flash lightly and try to walk him around me. I will stay here in the center. I will pivot with his moves," José called to her.

Clara nudged Flash slightly, but instead of walking he began running.

Jerked instantly to the ground, José began being pulled behind Flash. "Stop him! Stop him!" José yelled from the ground as he tried to stop the dirt from going into his nostrils and mouth. The rope dug deeply into his hands and ripped his skin open. Blood trickled slowly from the slits of skin. Dirt and small pebbles quickly embedded the fresh wounds, adding to the pain and burning the flesh as if he had touched a hot branding iron.

Clara pulled tightly back on the reins and yelled, "Whoa!" Flash stopped immediately to her command. Clara saw José on the ground and yelled, "José, are you all right? Shall I come and help you up?"

José shook his head and pulled himself to his feet and walked backward from Clara and Flash until the rope became taut again between him and them. "Señorita, climb down from the saddle and hold the reins in your right hand while standing by Flash's neck on his left side," he called to her.

Clara, again, did what José told her to do.

"Now, Flash, we will try this again," José, said. Motioning to Clara, he said, "Give him a smooching sound and say 'walk' loudly and firmly. At the same time, you begin to walk to signal him."

Clara looked over Flash's withers at José and nodded in agreement to his instructions. With her lips held tightly together, Clara sucked in warm air and let out a long rusty-door-hinge screech. She quickly said, "Walk," loudly and firmly as José had said. At the same time, she put her right foot forward and began to walk. Flash followed her quietly. They walked a full circle around José before he said anything. He called to her, "Señorita, say "Whoa," and stop walking at the same time."

Clara did as he told her, and she and Flash came to a stop.

"Very good, Flash!" José exclaimed. "Señorita, let's try this again."

For the rest of the afternoon Flash and Clara walked around José, stopping only when told. She continued using the voice commands "Walk" and "Whoa" as she moved and stopped.

As she got ready to head for home, José said, "Tomorrow we will do the same as today, but Flash will have to do it without you leading him."

Clara was so proud of Flash that she kissed him several times on his soft nose. She thought he had done quite well with his first official lesson. She felt really sorry about José's hands. It must have really hurt, but he never let on that it did. She scolded Flash on the way home and told him he had to be more careful. "José is trying to help us, Flash, and you dragging him around like that wasn't very nice. We need José's help. If you don't mind your manners, he might quit working with us. That would leave us in a terrible fix, because I think he really knows what he is doing with you."

Flash bobbed his head up and down in agreement with her words. Clara day-dreamed the rest of the way home. A daydream that extended into the next day and caused Clara great embarrassment.

Chapter 12
Hazardous Thoughts

Clara tapped her fingers on her desk as she waited for the teacher, Miss Simpson, to give the instructions. The tapping rhythm seemed to gradually draw her away from the classroom and into Flash's saddle. Suddenly, she rode him, gliding smoothly over the open fields like warm caramel running slowly down the sides of a crisp apple. The gentle spring air filled her being with its freshness. The untamed wind caught her hair, snapping it unforgivably at the world.

"Clara! Clara, are you with us, child?" Miss Simpson asked, hovering over Clara's desk.

"Oh, I'm sorry, Miss Simpson, I was just thinking about..., oh never mind," Clara stammered, embarrassed that she 'd been caught daydreaming during class.

"As I was saying, class, we've only just a few weeks of school left before our summer recess. We will celebrate with an ice cream social on the last day. All the girls who are fourteen and older will bring picnic lunches to auction. We need to plan the games. I was thinking of horseshoes, and the three legged race. What other games do you want to play?" Miss Simpson asked.

Many of the children raised their hands. Miss Simpson began writing the games on the chalk board. Clara had a hard time concentrating on the discussion. She was eager to be out of the classroom and Mrs. Miller's shop and on Flash's back. Finally, Miss Simpson excused the children for the day.

Clara rushed past all the other students and hurried toward Mrs. Miller's shop. The ringing bell from the opening door woke Bezzie. He opened one eye just wide enough to see Clara. After a big yawn, he closed his eye and resumed his nap.

Mrs. Miller greeted Clara with a warm smile and hello. She told Clara that they had many more patterns to pin and cut today. She took Clara to the big table and showed her how to measure out the material from each bolt according to the longest piece of the pattern.

Clara first chose a deep green material. It reminded her of the lush green grass that grew next to the mountain rivers. It was almost black with its dark green velvet texture. The pattern was for a beautiful dress. Its sleeves were long and tight from the elbow down, with many small pearl buttons. From the elbow up, the sleeve puffed out like the sails of a ship. Its waistline was gathered and sewn tightly and outlined with a thick woven cord. Its bodice was covered with white pineapple lace, which made the dress even more beautiful. Mrs. Miller stood next to Clara as she began to measure out the material.

Clara held the bolt close to her chest and began to unroll the material with her outstretched hand, pulling it the full length of her arm. She unrolled four lengths of material and then looked at Mrs. Miller for approval before cutting the material. Mrs. Miller smiled and nodded.

"Mrs. Miller, if you don't mind my asking, who is this beautiful dress for?" Clara asked, cutting through the doubled thickness of material.

"I don't mind, Clara. It is for Mrs. Wilkinson. It's really going to be beautiful, isn't it?" Mrs. Miller asked.

"Yes, very beautiful. I don't really care for dresses, though. They just don't suit me for the things that I like to do," Clara replied.

"You're right. Sometimes dresses are just too, well, too big and bulky," Mrs. Miller agreed.

"What does Mrs. Wilkinson need such a fine dress like this for, Mrs. Miller?" she asked.

"Well, one of her daughters is having an engagement party at the end of this month. If you think this dress is beautiful, wait until you see the engaged daughter's dress. It is made of fine silk, which was imported from China. We not only have to make dresses for Mrs. Wilkinson and her daughter, but also for the other two daughters, and Mrs. Wilkinson's sister and nieces."

"It sounds like it is going to be quite an event, indeed," Clara said, completing the cutting.

"Wilkinsons don't spare any money when it comes to clothing the women of the household. They sure keep me busy and I'm very grateful for it. We've a big order, so we must get started pinning the patterns," Mrs. Miller said, pulling out a box of straight pins.

She reminded Clara to turn the material inside out before pinning the pattern to the material. She showed her how to line the pattern up straight against the fold for the pieces that needed doubling in size. "After you have all of the pieces cut out, Clara, please begin to pin the seams together."

Clara became so absorbed in her pinning that she never thought again about racing home to jump on Flash's back for his afternoon lesson. With the pinning done, she called for Mrs. Miller to inspect it before she began to cut out the pattern. Mrs. Miller placed her hand on Clara's shoulder and complimented her on a splendid job. It had been a long time since Clara had felt such a loving touch. It was a touch that Clara could feel in her heart. She was very pleased that Mrs. Miller was such a kind woman.

With Mrs. Miller's approval, Clara began cutting the dress one piece at a time. Before she knew it, the clock chimed five o'clock. Mrs. Miller came to the front of the shop to say good-bye to Clara.

She waved at her father as she ran past the jail toward home. She quickly changed and went to the barn to get Flash. He was waiting for her. She shared her apple with him, as always. Once in the saddle, she nudged him and he raced toward their meeting with José.

José greeted them as they rode up. "Hello, my friend! Flash, I see you are in a big hurry today to take your lesson."

Flash nodded his head up and down and acted as if he enjoyed the rubbing José was giving him. "Today we take the saddle off him and see if he remembers yesterday's voice commands without you leading him," José said, turning toward Clara.

"Okay, Flash! You heard the teacher! Off with that saddle!" Clara said, laughing, as she pulled loose the cinch and grabbed the saddle, lowering it from his back.

José took off the bridle and placed the long rope around his head and nose like the halter he had made yesterday. "Okay, big Flash, Clara and I are going to walk away from you and you stand here. Flash was busy grazing, so he didn't seem to notice that José and Clara had moved away from him. José continued backing until the rope he held in his hand was tight. He took his sombrero off with his free hand and began waving it in a circular motion.

Flash looked up at José's movement. As Flash's eyes met José's, José clicked with his tongue and made a smooching sound and said, "Walk," very loudly. Flash put his left foot forward and hesitated, looking back at José. José again made the clicking and smooching sounds and said, "Walk!" in a louder command. Flash then began to walk in a circle around José. Every few steps he would look toward José as if to get his signal to continue.

Clara was thrilled with Flash's behavior! She began patting José on the back and saying, "You're the greatest horse trainer I have ever met, and Flash is the smartest horse on earth."

"Señorita, I do appreciate your compliments, but we have just begun. There is much more to do. I agree that this Flash is a smart one, though. He understands much of what is said. He just chooses to respond to it in his own manner."

The rest of the lesson continued smoothly. Eventually Flash didn't look at José for instructions.

He waited until José told him to "Whoa!" or "Walk!" "Tomorrow we will try this with the saddle and you on his back. We will try to coordinate a light pressure of your heel at the same time and see if he connects the nudge with the voice command for walk," José said to Clara as he walked up to Flash to remove the rope.

Clara, with José's help, put Flash's saddle and bridle back on him. "I'll meet you here tomorrow at the same time," Clara said, turning Flash toward home.

She braced herself and then nudged Flash lightly with her heel. Flash immediately obeyed and sprang forward and sped toward home. Clara loved the feeling of complete freedom when she allowed Flash to run wild. She didn't feel as if she had to control her thoughts, feelings, or actions when she and Flash raced. She thought that perhaps this is what it felt like to be an eagle.

They ran over the familiar ground toward home. Clara looked up over Flash's head and could see the beautiful, full, bright orange sunset. It looked as if the sun were setting right on the edge of the earth. "I'd like to ride to the setting sun and walk right into its shining splendor. Its rays would reach deep into my heart and fill me with bright orange slices of light. I would always be happy with all that light inside me," she whispered, unaware of the sadness she would soon cause another.

Chapter 13
Branded Attraction

The days blended into weeks. It was hard for Clara to believe there were only three more days of school. Miss Simpson spent much of her time preparing them for the final exam. The results of the exam played an important part in being passed into the next grade. Even though her father had not supported her dream, she still worked hard for above passing grades. She knew it would make a big difference in entering college. She could not understand why he didn't think it was becoming of a lady to be an animal doctor. There were many things that her father didn't think becoming of a lady, and she had managed to do almost all of them. Not really out of spite; it just happened naturally.

While most girls Clara's age spent their days cooking pies and mending clothes, Clara had gone out with Pete, branding cattle and mending fences. Sheriff Browning would say, "Clara, it just ain't becoming of a lady to be out wrestling cattle to the ground. Besides, it is dangerous and it just ain't right having a small girl like you in such a dangerous predicament." Clara had laughed at her father's concern and reassured him that she was very careful; always under the watchful eye of Pete. It had never done any good for the sheriff to argue with Clara when it came to matters of this nature, because Clara always won with Pete on her side, persuading the sheriff to allow her to join him.

In all the years that Clara spent on the range with Pete, she saw many calves die suddenly, for no apparent reason. She felt sad and wanted to help them, but Pete would just shake his head and say, "Ain't nothing any of us can do. Its God's way of feeding the hungry in the wild."

Clara didn't agree. There was plenty in the wild to feed the wild. She had decided that she would get some animal doctor training and then she would be able to prevent so many calves from dying needlessly. There were many other suffering animals that she wanted to help, too. She had made up her mind many years ago. *Once Clara's mind is made up, there's no changing it.* That had been her father's favorite saying, because he believed it to be true.

Miss Simpson said they had studied enough for one day. "Now, children, we need to discuss our final preparations for the ice cream social." The older girls were all smiling and giggling. Clara supposed it had to do with the picnic baskets they were to make and auction. What a dumb idea she thought. *"Why should I pack a picnic lunch and auction it to share it with some dumb old boy?"* she wondered almost aloud.

Miss Simpson said the money from the baskets was going to buy some new entertaining books. "Reading just for pure delight," were Miss Simpson's exact words. Clara couldn't deny that having some books for reading pleasure was a good idea. "Well, I'll pack a lunch, but I better not get stuck with some awful boy to share it with," she mumbled to herself.

When class dismissed, Clara rushed toward
Mrs. Miller's shop. She raced through the door
without glancing up, and ran right into Matthew
Miller. She lifted her chin high to see his square
jaw. He was so tall! She couldn't believe it was
Matthew. "I'm very sorry, Matthew," she managed
to mutter quietly.

"No harm done, Clara. You are just a little
spit of a thing. Your running into me ain't going to
cause me harm," he laughed looking fully into her
face.

"Clara," Mrs. Miller interrupted, "Matthew's
come in to drive you out to the Wilkinson's to
deliver the dresses. I didn't want to leave the shop
unattended for that length of time, and one of us
needs to go and make sure that all the dresses fit
properly."

Before speaking, Clara gulped and let the
wetness in her throat flow slowly downward.
"Well, Mrs. Miller, we won't need to bother
Matthew. I'm completely capable of driving the
team out to the Wilkinson's myself."

"I'm sure you are, Clara, but the sheriff
warned us that we should travel in pairs if going too
far out of town. Those Brewster brothers robbed
another bank in the territory, and he isn't taking any
chances," Mrs. Miller replied.

"Well, then, Mrs. Miller, you go ahead with
Matthew. You should be there to fit the dresses.
You know much more about it than I do. I'll stay
and mind the shop for you."

"Thank you for the offer, but I have a patron
coming in soon for some special fittings that I need

to attend to myself. Don't be afraid, Clara, Matthew will take perfectly good care of you. He won't let anything happen to you."

"Silly woman! I'm not afraid to ride out there because of some dumb old bank robbers. And I surely don't need Matthew to take care of me. I can take care of myself," she thought to herself, while trying to smile at Mrs. Miller. "Very well, Mrs. Miller, as you wish. We will get going with the dresses," Clara said, turning toward the back of the shop.

Clara picked up the dresses and pushed past Matthew. Matthew, who was not in favor of taking Clara, followed her out of the shop. She laid the dresses in the wagon and covered them with the dust cloth that Mrs. Miller handed her. "Don't fret none, Ma, we'll be just fine. I'll be back to pick you up before sunset," Matthew said to Mrs. Miller, as she stood in the doorway of the shop looking worried.

Clara climbed into the rig and sat next to Matthew. He lifted the reins and gave them a gentle crack and told the team to move on. They quickly responded to his command and started down the street. Clara's father was coming down the street toward them. "Hold up there for a minute, Matthew," he yelled out, waving his hand as he stepped into the street. "Now, you be careful out there, son. I know you are a good driver and a good shot. Just keep your eyes open. If anything spooks you, try to outrun it instead of using your gun."

Matthew was instantly mad. "I'm not your son and I don't spook easily. I ain't for running. That's for yellow bellied cowards."

"Easy, Matthew, I didn't mean to imply that you were spooked easily. I'm just a mite concerned, that's all. Just be careful and pay close attention to what's around you. We'll be expecting you before sunset," Sheriff Browning said, patting Clara's hand and smiling at her.

"Boy, you sure are hotheaded, Matthew Miller," Clara blurted in his direction.

"Well, you just figure how you would feel if the man that killed your father called you 'son'! Now, let's just forget it and get on with our business," Matthew said disgustedly.

Clara and Matthew rode in an uncomfortable silence. Clouds of dust billowed behind them making it impossible to see anything in back of them. Matthew handled the horses with great skill. Clara saw his muscular arms bulging out through his shirt. His broad shoulders were erect and proud. The red handkerchief he wore tied around his neck lifted slightly with the breeze, causing his hair to turn up into a shapeless flip on his shoulders. His blue eyes stared forward and occasionally darted to the sides. It was hard for Clara to decide if they were clear blue as the sky, or more solid like the mountain rivers. She didn't have the right angle for looking deep into them. Even if she did, she knew she wouldn't dare gaze into this boy's eyes. His thick heavy legs stayed steady even over the rough road. She knew that they were as solid as a rock. She figured he could walk a hundred miles without tiring on legs like that. She finally summed it all up in one word: "Handsome."

"What did you say?" Matthew asked her.

Oh dear! She was embarrassed! She didn't realize she had said it out loud. "I said, "Have some," she stammered holding out the canteen to him.

Matthew took a long, hard drink of the cool water Clara offered him. It was refreshing, washing the dust down his throat. He turned toward her to hand back the canteen. He had not realized until this very moment how attractive she was. Her small, delicate face splattered with deer hide-colored freckles complimented her small nose that had the slightest tip to it. Her hair glistened. Its color reminded him of the shiny fur of a fox. It wasn't bright red, but it wasn't a dull red either. She seemed so small sitting next to him. Her small hands reached to catch her bonnet as it flew backward and was caught by the ribbons around her slender, white neck. If she were a filly, she couldn't be any prettier. He would have to admit she was: "Pretty."

Clara looked at Matthew and asked, "What did you say?"

"Pretty. The mountains, aren't they pretty?" he stammered, wishing he had kept his mouth shut.

During the rest of the ride, they both stole glances at each other and silently admired what they were seeing.

Reaching Wilkinson's ranch, Clara saw José coming up toward the barns. She waved to him and said, "José. Good day! I had hoped to see you. I'll not be able to work with Flash today, because I'm here with the ladies' dresses for fittings."

"Okay, señorita. I look forward to tomorrow. Flash is doing so well. He will win that race."

"I agree with you, José. You have done such a wonderful job with Flash. I'll never be able to thank you enough," Clara said with a big smile.

"Oh, señorita, you flatter me. You will win the race and I will get to train horses. That will be enough thanks for me. I have to get back to work now. It was nice to see you, señorita."

"Dear me, where are my manners? José, before you leave, I'd like to introduce you to Matthew Miller."

José reached his hand up toward Matthew to shake it. Matthew's hand met José's in a sturdy shake. "So tell me, José, are you training Flash for the big race to ride him in it?"

"No señor, I'm not going to ride him in the race. Miss Clara, she plans to ride him. Never have I seen a better rider than Miss Clara. She fits on Flash like your glove does on your hand. They were born to be together," José replied, proudly.

"You really think that Clara and Flash have a good chance to win this race?" Matthew asked.

"Oh, yes, señor! A very good chance. If I were to bet any money, I would put it on them."

"Well, obviously you didn't know that females are not permitted to ride in the race. Guess Clara will have to find another glove to fit on the hand for this one," Matthew smirked, as he jumped down from the wagon.

José walked back toward and barn and slipped out of sight. Clara looked at Matthew and stuck her tongue out at him, the whole time thinking what a pig-headed fool he was. Who did he think he was? Some big important man telling José that girls couldn't ride in the race. "Well, Master Miller, I'll show you who is going to win that race and it's not going to be some farm boy!" she seethed between clenched teeth.

Matthew let Clara walk ahead of him to the door. Watching her struggle to keep the dresses in her arms, he wondered how such a little mite thought she could possibly win the Mt. Franklin Race. *"She really must be a dreamer. Somebody ought to take those silly dreams out of her empty little head before she gets hurt,"* he thought.

Once Clara stepped inside the Wilkinson's magnificent house, she forgot all about her anger toward Matthew. The wooden floors shined so that her face stared back at her. Sitting in an hourglass shaped pale, pink vase were the most beautiful, fully opened tulips that she had ever seen. The round-topped table in the foyer holding the vase had mountain lion claws carved at the base of its legs.

Mrs. Wilkinson came at once to greet her and Matthew. "Please join us upstairs, Clara. Matthew, you may wait in the parlor. I'll have some lemonade brought to you," Mrs. Wilkinson said, looking at him.

"Thank you Ma'am, but I'm going to go out and look at those fine animals of your husband's," he replied.

"Very well, Matthew. We'll find you when we are finished," Mrs. Wilkinson said, leading Clara up the wide, open staircase. Green ivy wound around the banner shooting between the spindles and wrapped the vines tightly like stretched elastic. Each step had beautiful paintings of flowers on it. By the time she reached the top step, every kind of flower she had known from picture books were represented in full color.

Clara followed Mrs. Wilkinson obediently. They reached a large room at the top of the stairs and went inside. There were six young women and a lady, close to Mrs. Wilkinson's age, Clara figured, sitting and talking excitedly. The young women all gathered around Clara looking for their dresses. The room's walls were papered with big pink flowered wallpaper. Clara had heard about wallpapered walls, but she had never seen any. The floor's huge rug matched the color of the flowers on the wall.

Clara didn't know which dress belonged to whom. It didn't matter. The women all knew which dress was theirs. They stripped away their dresses and were all in their petticoats before Clara could open the small basket Mrs. Miller had given her containing measuring tape and straight pins.

The room bustled with excitement! The girls laughed and danced about in their new dresses. Some practiced curtseying while pretending they had petite fans in their hands. They laughed and said, "May I have this dance, Miss," to each other. Clara thought they were silly making such fools of themselves over the idea of dancing with boys!

As she admired herself in the looking glass, Mrs. Wilkinson said, "My dress fits me just wonderfully. Please tell Mrs. Miller how absolutely beautiful it is and how much I admire her workmanship."

Clara nodded and agreed to take the message back to Mrs. Miller. Mrs. Wilkinson's sister looked marvelous in her royal blue velvet dress. Clara instantly knew they were sisters, because they looked so much alike.

Clara hemmed two of the dresses with the pins Mrs. Miller sent. Darla, the engaged daughter, needed the waistline of her silk dress taken in almost a full inch. Clara made the adjustments quite easily, to her surprise, and pinned the dress according to where the waist needed to be taken in. Within an hour the same young women who danced around the room in delight in their party gowns had taken them off and were back into their neatly pressed cotton dresses.

Clara took the three dresses with her for the necessary alterations and went in search of Matthew. He sat on the porch with Mr. Wilkinson, talking about horses and racing. Matthew introduced Clara to Mr. Wilkinson as she stepped out onto the porch. He was a big man. Clara figured he stood as tall as her father. She thought he may be a little older as his hair was gray around the tops of his ears and a little thinner than her father's.

"Well, we best be heading back to town," Matthew stated matter of factly as he rose.

The wagon moved along the road at a steady pace. The sun started to make its descent in the western sky. It cast a melon glow around the sky adjoining it. Slight colors of pink seeped silently through small wispy clouds above the huge round sun. Neither Matthew or Clara spoke.

Finally Matthew broke the silence with a gruff statement. "Clara, you better stop telling people you are going to ride Flash in the race. You know girls are not allowed to ride in it, and you are just making a little fool of yourself telling people otherwise."

"Well, Matthew Miller, you smug, overgrown boy, just who do you think you are, telling me what I ought or ought not be doing? It is none of your business what my intentions are. I'll expect you to mind your own business and keep out of my affairs!" she yelled at him.

"Oh! Who is smug around here? It sure ain't me! It's too dangerous for any woman to ride in that race! You'd get lost the first night out there! Your father wouldn't be there to find you and wipe your nose for you, either! You best keep on learning woman stuff with my ma and forget about that race!" he yelled back at her loudly.

"Woman stuff! What in tarnation are you talking about, Matthew Miller? I'm not doing any more woman stuff than I absolutely have to! Besides I've been working with your mother so I can earn the money I need for...never you mind what I'm doing! It just isn't any of your business!"

"Oh, come on Clara! You know darned well my ma's been hired by your father to teach you women fixings. So get off your high horse and stop acting too big for your britches!"

"I don't know what you are talking about, you big bully! Your ma pays me to work in her shop. She needed help and my father suggested that I try the job. That's what happened and you know it!" she screamed.

"You aren't only too big for your britches, but you're downright stupid, too! You just ask your father how you got that job. He'll tell you. That is unless he is a liar as well as a murderer."

"You take that back, Matthew Miller, or I'll shoot you right here and now with your own gun!" Clara screamed holding Matthew's rifle in her hands.

"Put that gun down, little Missy, before you hurt yourself with it," Matthew laughed.

"I mean it, Matthew Miller! You take back what you said about my father right now, or I'll be driving this here rig on into town with one dead, overgrown farm boy in it!" she yelled.

"Well, if it will shut your screaming up and give me a peaceful ride the rest of the way home, I'll oblige and tell you I take back what I said about your pa. Now give me my gun and sit over there and behave like a lady. That is, if you know how to behave like a lady."

"Lady or no lady, Matthew Miller, you are a downright dirty scoundrel! And I'm sure glad that I don't have to put up with the likes of you in school." Clara knew as soon as she said it she shouldn't have. That was what her father had often tried to tell her about hurtful words. Once you say them you cannot take them back. They have done their damage and caused the pain you intended. *"Well, he deserved it,"* she thought. Even so, it didn't give her any comfort.

She looked over at Matthew and his face looked drained of its natural color. He looked grayer and older somehow. He looked very serious now.

She knew that she had hurt him badly. He wouldn't admit it, even if she apologized. She figured there was nothing else she could do but keep quiet for the rest of the ride home.

Sheriff Browning met them just outside town. "Well, Matthew, I knew I could rely on you to bring my little Clara home safe. I'll be taking her off your hands now. Your ma is waiting for you." Clara jumped out of the rig and her father pulled her up behind him onto the horse with powerful, strong arms.

She looked over at Matthew and said, "Thank you, Matthew, I'm sorry if I hurt your feelings. I was mad and I tend to say things out of turn when I'm angry."

"Never you mind, Clara Browning. You didn't hurt my feelings none," he said as he pulled the wagon away.

"So, Clara, what did you say to Matthew that you should not have said to him?" her father inquired.

"It doesn't really matter, Father. I just shouldn't have said it, that's all," she said, laying her cheek against her father's back.

Clara forgot what Matthew had said about his ma teaching her woman stuff and her father paying for her teachings until she was clearing the dishes away from the table that night.

Her father sat on the porch watching fireflies. "Aren't they a sight, Clara?" he asked, pointing to one of them as she stepped out to join him.

"They are that. It's like they carry their own candlewick with them to light their way, so they don't get lost in the dark. Father, Matthew told me that you hired Mrs. Miller to teach me some woman doings. I told him he didn't know what he was talking about. Why do you suppose he would say such a cruel thing to me?"

"It may sound cruel, Clara, but it wasn't intended to be," he said, turning toward her.

"What? What do you mean, Father? Is it true what Matthew told me? You had to pay Mrs. Miller to hire me? No wonder she is so pleasant to me. She's making sure she earns her money. I'll not step one foot in that shop ever again, you can just be certain of that!" she cried, knowing how much she would miss Mrs. Miller's company and kindness. It didn't matter now, though. It was all a big show to earn her some extra money.

"Now, just hold on there, Clara. Don't get yourself worked up into a fit. It started like that. I had gotten concerned with your birthday coming on that you needed to learn some sewing, cooking, and

the like. I asked Mrs. Miller to help teach you the
sewing part. I arranged to pay her for her service.
But after the first week you were there, she refused
to accept any money. She said you were a big help
to her and she would pay your wages herself.
Matthew told you to hurt you, because of me."

"You just wait until I see that big bully!
Next time I won't put the gun down, I'll just shoot
him!" she wailed. Turning to leave she realized she
had opened her mouth again when she shouldn't
have.

"What are you talking about, guns and
shooting? What went on today?" her father
demanded.

" I had just a little trouble with that bully.
He said something about you that I didn't like. So I
made him apologize at gunpoint. I had his gun.
That made it even worse, don't you think?" she
asked, laughing, hoping her father would see the
humor in the situation. Of course, he didn't.

"Clara Abigail Browning! Sometimes I
think you are the most pig-headed child on the face
of this earth! Don't you ever threaten somebody
with a gun! You cannot imagine the horror it is to
take another man's life! It doesn't matter what that
person did. It doesn't seem to justify the sickness
you carry around in your gut for the rest of your
life. Now, I suggest that you march into that house
and go to bed before I do something we will both
regret."

Clara wasted no time obeying her father. In
her room, she slipped out of her dress and climbed
into the safety of her bed. She lay in the darkness

knowing she deserved her father's wrath tonight, but she never expected the depth of his wrath that she encountered within the next week.

Chapter 14
The Breeches

The next morning the sun shone so brightly that Clara pulled her bonnet rim tight down over her eyes to prevent the sun from making them water. She walked up the familiar school steps and entered through the big, dark, wooden doors. Soon just church services would use the building for the summer. She wouldn't miss the Friday ritual of taking the small tables to the back of the room and stacking them for church on Sunday. The men always put the tables back on Sunday after service to set the class room for Monday morning. Miss Simpson came into the room with an armful of papers. Clara knew they were the final exams. For the past few weeks, she had studied and paid close attention the best she could. But still taking a final exam made her nervous. She felt her left eyelid twitch a little bit. The twitching became noticeable whenever Clara was nervous about something. It felt like her pulse. The steady twitching pattern pulled her eyelid toward the outside of her face.

"Children," Miss Simpson called. "Everyone be seated now."

Some younger boys came rushing into the building, slamming into each other and rocking the tables as they shoved their bodies abruptly behind them. Miss Simpson scolded them.

"When you finish your exam, please leave the classroom and go out to the tables set up outside and wait for Mrs. Henderson. She will supervise the decoration making for our party. Tomorrow I will go over your exam results with each of you and then we will finish making preparations for the celebration.

Clara's eye twitched at a much faster pace. It really annoyed her, but there wasn't anything she could do about it. Miss Simpson passed out the exams. Clara turned hers over and read the instructions. The first section was math. Since math was her favorite subject, it made her feel confident in answering the questions.

After some time passed, Clara noticed a few students her age were missing. "Oh, Clara, that means the exam isn't has hard as you're making it," she fussed to herself.

She decided to ignore the fact that others had left and concentrate on the questions. The large round wooden clock on the wall loudly ticked off one minute at a time until its hands announced half past eleven. As its minute hand reached the six, Clara stood up and took her exam papers up to Miss Simpson.

She stepped outside and the sun stood almost straight above her. It still glared brightly. She lifted her bonnet and placed it snugly on her head to shade her eyes and face. She tied it around her thin neck and finished the tie with a big bow. She didn't like bonnets anymore than she did dresses, but they had their purpose.

Mrs. Henderson excused them for the day an hour early. Clara gladly reached Mrs. Miller's shop earlier than usual. She wanted to talk to her about making a pair of pants to fit her snug around her butt and thighs. If she could make a pair tight like that, she knew they wouldn't slide up on her and cause sore spots from rubbing against her skin in the saddle.

Busy with a customer, Mrs. Miller glanced up and smiled at Clara when she walked in. Clara went to the back of the shop and greeted Bezzie, as was now her custom. She started going through the different bolts of material. Looking for a heavier weight material, she found the dark blue denim used for men's overalls. She began drawing a pattern on a piece of paper for the riding pants she had in mind. Mrs. Miller walked up behind her and asked her what she was working on. Clara explained to Mrs. Miller that she needed better fitting riding pants. The others she had were too loose and caused sore spots on her buttocks and legs.

Mrs. Miller saw a flicker of excitement in Clara's eyes when she spoke. She had a feeling that Clara had gotten herself involved in something slightly dishonest. "Do you ride your horse often?" she asked her, probingly.

"Yes, quite often. I'm training him with the help of a friend," she answered unsuspecting.

"Do you ride side saddle?"

"Heavens no! Side saddle suits grown-up women and sissies. I sit astride like the men do. That's one thing, I must admit, men do right!" Clara said giggling.

Mrs. Miller laughed with Clara. She always spoke honestly about her thoughts and feelings. The sheriff had stopped by on many occasions to check on Clara's progress. He had never come when Clara was at the shop. Mrs. Miller knew he didn't want Clara to know he had checked on her. Clara quickly learned everything that Mrs. Miller had taught her. Mrs. Miller enjoyed having Clara around, because she was always happy and laughing about the simplest things. She felt guilty that she assumed Clara was up to something she shouldn't be, so she stopped questioning her.

Mrs. Miller decided to help Clara with her tight fitting pants. "What you really need, Clara, is riding breeches. Lighter weight pants made from material that moves and stretches with you, but not out of shape to cause the looseness. I had some of that material here in the shop."

Mrs. Miller jumped up before Clara could get out of her chair and began looking behind the counter for the material. She came back with some desert sand colored material. Handing it to Clara she said, "Making them tight everywhere, including around the calves of your legs and ankles, creates the best riding pants. If they are tight, they won't ride up on you and cause the wrinkles that rub against your skin."

"Thank you, Mrs. Miller. What do I owe you?" Clara asked.

"You don't owe me anything, Clara. Shall we see what we can come up with on that contraption of mine?" she asked teasingly.

Mrs. Miller and Clara worked on the pants that afternoon and had them finished before Clara left to meet José. Clara tried them on. They fit her tightly everywhere. Mrs. Miller had put foot straps at the bottom of them. They slid under Clara's feet.

The straps guaranteed that the pant legs wouldn't ride up on Clara.

Clara was more excited than usual about working with Flash and José this afternoon. Every day became warmer. Delicate, bleached yellow wild daisies danced behind the tall veils of prairie grass along the path Clara traveled toward home. She called for Flash, as she strode up the lane. He dashed forward, whinnying and snorting. He lifted himself so high and erect on his back legs that he looked like a marble statue. His head bounced simultaneously with the movement of his front legs thrashing forward in greeting. Clara could not wait to feel him, so she ran to the corral and climbed over the board fence. Catching her long dress on a nail, she tore it the full length from her hip to the hem line. As she jerked the material to pull it loose, she lost her balance and fell head first into the corral. Flash walked over to her and nudged her with his nose and snorted. Clara rolled over and looked up at the animal she loved more than anything else in life and began to laugh. "What a hilarious sight this must be," she giggled to Flash.

She pushed herself up with her hands and wrapped her arms around Flash's neck. His hair was damp from sweat. His hot, steamy breath and the leathery odor of his perspiration filled her nostrils. She breathed in deeply the musty smell that she had always loved. She held his nose tightly between her two hands and kissed his soft muzzle with her tender lips. His whiskers tickled her cheeks, as she caressed him with her full face.

She stood back and admired his perfect beauty. "I'll be back as soon as I get changed," she said, stroking his neck.

She laid the torn dress on her bed beside the breeches. She surveyed the damage and decided that she'd be able to repair the dress at the shop. She pulled and jerked into the breeches with some difficulty. She tugged an inch at a time on the legs to get them on. She wiggled and twisted around getting her butt into them. She pushed her arms hurriedly into the sleeves of a cotton shirt. She tucked the shirt inside the breeches. This left her little room for her fingers between her stomach, the buttons, and button holes of the breeches. She sucked a deep breath and made enough room to slip her fingers inside to button them up. She squatted down and bounced back up a few times adjusting the material to a perfect fit around her.

She replaced her bonnet with her leather hat. She dashed out the door with an apple in her mouth while she pulled her gloves over her small hands. José had insisted that she wear gloves while riding Flash. He had said the gloves instead of human skin when touching a horse reduces the horse's misunderstanding of friend and horse versus master and horse. Clara didn't argue with José's techniques. He had taught her and Flash much more than she had ever dreamed in the short six weeks possible.

She galloped toward the foothills. Clara looked at the rising limestone plateaus. Their pale purple and pink soft layers of color separated by gray thin slabs looked so safe and secure hidden among their massiveness. She had often wondered how something so big and alarming could be so tender and beautiful to gaze at.

At first, she seemed to slide in the saddle from the weaving fibers of the new breeches. But the longer she rode, the more they felt as if they were a part of her skin, not giving one inch to wrinkles. The material held her knees so tightly that her knee cap protruded upward from her flesh. This caused a safe, secure feeling, having her skin pulled tight like a braided rope.

José greeted them with a big smile and nod. "Señorita, there is little for me to teach you now. Flash learned quickly. He obeys your body and voice commands without hesitation. I can tell he still wants to run fast all the time, but he does respect your authority. Today I want to teach you how to care for him in the mountains."

Clara nodded in agreement. "Very well, José, What do I need to know?" she asked.

"The air in the mountains is much thinner than here. You'll need to keep him in a steady gait. Long strides are better than short choppy ones. The more up and down muscular movements increase the chances of cramping muscles. Long, straight, fluid, forward strides stretch the muscles outward. You must always watch the terrain. You are responsible for guiding him over the safest, level ground possible. There are a few dangerous cactus up there. Make sure you keep him a safe distance from them. Thorns, in horse flesh unattended, can be deadly."

That statement concerned Clara. She asked, "How do I know if he has picked up a thorn?"

"Each night go over his entire body with the palm of your hand. Check up and down his legs, too. If you feel one, pull it out. Make sure you carry salve with you. It will be fine if you check daily and put salve on the wounds. Do not allow him to eat during the day. Let him graze in the evening as much as he wants to. There are not many water holes in that area. Always let him drink when you can. Only let him drink from your water supply if he goes an entire day and night without water. He can go much longer than you without water. If you get desperate, cut open cactus and drink its liquid. Make sure several times a day that you clean his hooves. Do you have any questions?" he asked.

"I believe I understand. Thank you, José, for all that you have done. We will win the race and make you and your father proud. I need your help buying the supplies. The store owner would get suspicious if I buy them. He'd tell my father," she replied.

"I'll go into town tomorrow. Do you know what you need?"

"I made a list," she said, handing him the list and money.

"Meet me here tomorrow at our regular time. I'll bring the supplies to you," he said, getting up to leave. He hesitated for a moment and turned back to her, "Señorita, I know we have discussed this before, but are you sure that you want to go through with this? Danger waits out there for riders. Your father will be angry, and I fear for your safety."

"I am sure. I want so much to go to veterinary school. My father will not send me. He doesn't believe in it. He most especially doesn't believe in a woman studying it. It is the only way. I know that Flash and I will be fine. We will win the race. Don't worry about me," she said, smiling up at him from where she sat on the ground, not suspecting the horrible dangers that waited for her.

Chapter 15
The Bank Robbery

Clara felt relieved when Miss Simpson told her she did very well on the exam. The last official day at school went by quickly. She dreaded tomorrow as much as she did taking the exam yesterday. The thought of making a lunch to auction disgusted her. "I wonder what dumb boy I'll get stuck with!" she spat into the air on her way to Mrs. Miller's that afternoon.

Suddenly, she was pushed to the ground with such harshness that she lost her breath. Her nose and lips ground into the dirt as somebody ran over her with heavy boots. She didn't dare move, because she heard gunfire and screaming all around her. She lay there trembling, wanting to look up. She fought the urge to lift her head and look as long as she could. Slowly, she lifted her forehead just enough so that she was resting on her chin. She saw the daylight surrounding her. She lay still for a moment before she continued. She tilted her head up until all of her head's weight rested on her chin. She could see running feet and horses hooves stomping all around her. She realized that she was lying in the street. This posed immediate danger. She slowly moved her arms that were tucked under her body. Quickly she extended her elbows outward from her body urgently sliding her hands across her hip bones. She pulled her hands upward parallel to her shoulders and turned her hands over so that her palms were against the ground. She thrust herself upward with great speed and force. On her knees, in a split second, she pushed herself backwards with her hands. She felt her feet under her and leaped up on them and ran toward the side of the street. Just as she reached the wooden sidewalk, a large group of riders raced over where she had been lying.

She felt soothing arms going around her shoulders. Clara turned to see Mrs. Miller behind her. "Come, Darling, let's get you inside," she commanded gently.

Mrs. Miller took Clara to the back of the shop and sat her down on the window seat. She unlaced Clara's boots and slid them from her feet. While asking Clara where she was hurt, she slowly ran her hand up Clara's legs to her knees. "Do your legs hurt anywhere, Clara?" she asked.

"No. My legs feel fine. My back hurts a little, though. My face hurts in some spots, too. What happened out there, Mrs. Miller?" she asked, trying not to cry from the pain.

"The bank was robbed. I suspect you got in the way of the fleeing thieves. Your face seems bruised and scratched up, but I'm more concerned about your back. Let's unbutton your dress and have a look," she said while getting behind Clara.

The pain grew worse as Clara sat there in the shop. She thought it would be better if she went home and laid down. Mrs. Miller fussed over her for quite some time. Finally, Clara convinced her that she was fine, but needed to go home. "Oh, dear, Clara, I wish your father were here to take you home. I suppose he'll be out chasing those thieves for some time before he comes back."

"I suppose he will be," Clara agreed.

The shop door burst open causing the bells to beat against the glass in the door. Matthew came bursting through the curtain that separated the front of the shop from the back of the shop. "Ma, are you all right?" he asked, out of breath.

"Why, Matthew, I'm just fine. Clara here, though, had quite a scare. She was caught up in the escape and was nearly trampled to death in the street," Mrs. Miller answered.

"The sheriff asked that every able-bodied man join the posse to run down those dirty Brewster Brothers. I'm fixin' to join them. Not that I'm obliged to help that murderin' sheriff none. But those robbers made off with all the race winnings. I need to help get that money back for the race next week, so I can win it."

Clara felt the anger building up in her throat as Matthew spoke. She wanted to knock him down and spit in his face. She respected Mrs. Miller too much to say anything, though. Besides, she felt rather lightheaded at the moment.

Clara woke up in the arms of Matthew Miller. Mrs. Miller stooped over them calmly telling Clara to wake up. Clara saw tears in Mrs. Miller's eyes as she slowly focused on her face.

Matthew's arms felt sturdy and strong around her. He sat cradling her in his lap as if she were a child. She pushed herself against him to try to sit up straight, but he held her tightly against his chest. "Now, child, don't struggle," Mrs. Miller said putting a cold cloth against her forehead.

The coolness felt good to Clara, so she eased back and tried to relax. "What happened?" she demanded in a hoarse whisper.

"You passed out and Matthew caught you," Mrs. Miller replied.

She turned her head. Her chin was resting against Matthew's huge chest. She lifted her eyes until she could see his face. She immediately felt caught up in a whirlwind when she saw her reflection in his eyes. It wasn't her reflection, but the vacuums caused when their eyes met. She dropped her gaze and then said, "Thank you, Matthew. I'm grateful to you."

"Was nothin', Clara. It happened, and I was here. Ma says we best be gettin' you home now, so you can rest. I'll take you there before I join your father and the others," he said, standing up with her still in his arms.

"Matthew Miller, I'll not have you carry me out on the street like I'm some baby. You put me down this instant," Clara demanded.

"Clara, stop being so darned pig-headed. I'm carrying you to the wagon and that's that," he bellowed back at her.

"The both of you quit your fussing. Clara, I'll come check on you later. Don't worry about fixing supper. I'll take care of that," Mrs. Miller said, as she followed them out into the street.

Matthew gently lifted Clara into the seat. Mrs. Miller patted her hand and smiled up at her. She called over to Matthew, "You be careful, Son.

88

I'll be waiting for your return." He smiled and nodded to his mother as they pulled out into the street.

Matthew hopped out of the wagon and ran to Clara's side before she could even muster up the strength to climb down. He had his one arm under her bottom and the other under her arms and around her back so quickly that he caught her off guard. "Matthew, you don't have to carry me into the house. I'm just fine now. Really!" she stammered.

"I ain't taking a chance of you passing out again. Just hush and tell me where you want me to lay you," he said gently.

"My room is just behind the kitchen. I'll rest in there," she answered softly. She decided there was no sense in arguing with him. She really didn't have the energy, anyway.

He put her on the bed and pulled the big soft pillow under her head. He took the extra blanket at the foot of her bed and placed it over her. "Is there anything else you need before I leave?" he asked.

"Just one thing. An answer from you. Why are you so fired up on winning that race next week? It's got to be more than just the money. What are you out to prove?" she asked.

"It really ain't your business, Clara Browning. I suspect this little accident prevents you from riding in the race. Good thing, too, it sure ain't a place for a girl anyway. I don't suppose your father had approved of your being in the race. Not that I care what that murderer wants or doesn't want!" he said rudely.

"Get out of my house, Matthew Miller, this instant, or I will shoot you where you stand!" she yelled.

He turned and briskly walked out of the room. She could hear his spurs ringing as he crossed the kitchen floor. The slamming door echoed his departure. He had left mad, too. That didn't bother Clara. She didn't like him anyway!

It surprised her how much it hurt to lift her legs when getting out of the bed the next morning. Clara's back felt so stiff that when she moved her spine stretched against its will. The pain shot up from her tailbone to her shoulders. Her muscles ached and throbbed like a toothache. She felt as if she had weights tied around her ankles pulling her legs out of their sockets whenever she took a step. She heard Jake talking with somebody in the kitchen. She slowly walked across her bedroom floor and opened the door. She stepped into the kitchen and saw José and Jake.

"José, What are you doing here?" she asked.

"I worried when you didn't come yesterday. I heard about the bank robbery last night. They said that you got hurt, Señorita. Are you okay?" he asked concerned.

"Yes, thank you, José. Thank you for coming by," she answered.

"I wondered about our business arrangement," he said, smiling over at Jake.

"Jake, please go get some fresh water," Clara said, turning in his direction.

After Jake left the house, Clara told José she would open her bedroom window. She told him to slide her supplies through it. José questioned Clara about whether she should still try to ride in the race. She didn't give him much chance to talk her out of it. Winning that race meant more than ever now. She aimed to prove to Matthew Miller that she could win the race. Being a girl wasn't a detriment, but a great asset!

Mrs. Miller knocked on the door just as José was reaching for the knob to go out. He bade her good morning and walked out after she stepped into the kitchen. He called from the porch that he would take care of the chores for her this morning and again this evening. Clara thanked him for his generosity.

Mrs. Miller began cracking eggs into a pan. "I've come to fix you and Jake some breakfast," she said tying an apron around her slender waist.

"Thank you for your generosity, too. I didn't realize just how many friends I had until now," Clara answered, sitting down at the table.

"I also packed your lunch for the social today. That is if you are up to going. It would be a shame for you to miss the big event that you've been waiting for all this month," Mrs. Miller giggled, knowing full well that Clara hated the idea of the party.

"I do plan to go. I want to help raise the money for the books Miss Simpson spoke of. So I will eat lunch with some stupid boy. I'll live through it. Thank you for packing the lunch," she said. She had no way of knowing she'd share it with the person she hated most.

Chapter 16
A Voice In the Crowd

Sheriff Browning and the posse had ridden hard all night. The Brewster brothers had split up and taken them high into the mountains. Many merchants complained about the harshness they endured during the chase. Early the next morning Sheriff Browning told them to head back to town. He knew the conditions would only worsen.

He asked for a volunteer to ride back to town and telegraph for a company of Texas Rangers. He knew this was a fight he couldn't win with a handful of townsmen. The messenger needed to wait for the Rangers and bring them to where the sheriff set up camp. Matthew stepped forward and volunteered. The sheriff explained the area where he planned to hole up until the Rangers joined him.

"Please check in on Clara and Jake for me. Tell her I feel just awful she was hurt yesterday. I'll see them soon," the sheriff said, walking Matthew to his horse.

Matthew agreed to carry his message home as he mounted Raven. Raven flew across the harsh, thirsty, rigid ground. Matthew guided him around cactus with tremendous ease. The dry sagebrush cracked helplessly under Raven's sturdy feet. Matthew saw the rooftops of El Paso as the noon sun began its ascent toward the center of the sky.

Reaching town, Matthew went straight to the telegraph office and sent the sheriff's request.

He then went to his mother's shop. Mrs. Miller gasped when she saw Matthew and said without taking a breath, "I'm so glad you're back. Are the robbers locked up? Is everyone all right? Where is the sheriff?"

"No, Ma. The robbers escaped high into the mountains. The posse rode back today. I've sent for some Rangers. I'll wait for their arrival. I'm to take them to the sheriff where he's holing up at," he answered, pouring a glass of water to wash down the dust caught in his throat.

"Are you headed to the ranch?" she asked without paying close attention. Her thoughts turned toward the mountains that harbored the sheriff. Suddenly his safety became extremely important to her, pressing deeply into her heart. The frequent visits he had paid her these past several weeks began flooding her mind. A focused tunnel of light had always exploded into an untamed glimmer in his eyes when he spoke of his passion for Texas. He had always spoken of Texas as if it were a woman. His wind-blown black hair had fallen aimlessly over his wide forehead when he had taken his hat off entering her shop. His large hands had seemed so gentle as they rolled the brim of his hat during their talks.

"Ma, Ma," Matthew yelled.

"Oh, dear. I'm sorry Matthew. What were you saying?" she asked confused.

"I asked if you would get a message to Clara from her father."

"She's at the school social. You run up there and give her the message. I cannot leave the shop now."

"Oh come on, Ma. I don't want to talk to her. She's so fire ornery all the time. I need to get to the ranch anyhow," he said, pleading like a little boy.

"Matthew Miller, you get on over to that school and give Clara her father's message," Mrs. Miller stated flatly and walked away.

"Fine!" he yelled, cramming his hat down on his head and stomping out.

Matthew spotted Clara right away. He walked up to her and asked to speak with her.

"Get lost you big bully!" she yelled.

"Clara Browning stop being so darn ugly for one minute and listen to me!" he yelled back at her.

"I wouldn't give you the time of day if you got on your knees and begged!" she yelled back, sticking her tongue out at him and rushing away.

"Gol-darn her. I've a mind to pick her up and dump her head first into the creek to cool her off," he muttered to himself.

Just then the preacher held up a picnic basket and announced Clara Browning packed it. "Who'll give me a quarter dollar...quarter dollar...quarter dollar...thank you, who'll give me a half dollar...half dollar...half dollar...," he auctioned in a fast tongue.

"I'll bid half dollar," a voice cried from the crowd.

"Do I have a dollar bid?" the preacher asked the crowd.

"Dollar!" another yelled from the crowd.

"Dollar-quarter!" the other voice called from behind the group of people.

"I'll take it for Dollar and a half," the less familiar voice shouted out again.

"Two dollars!" the voice most of the crowd recognized yelled determinedly.

"Do I have two dollars and a quarter?" the preacher asked the other bidder.

The bidder nodded yes with the brim of his sombrero.

"Do I have two dollars and a half?" the preacher turned and asked the young rancher.

The young rancher did not make an agreeing gesture. The preacher called out, Two dollars and a quarter, going once, going twice--!"

"Two dollars and a half!" the young rancher yelled lifting the brim of his leather hat.

The preacher asked, "Who'll pay three dollars?"

The crowd stood silent. Disbelief filled the air that the basket went for so much money. Who would pay such a price, many of them questioned?

Chapter 17
"Matthew Miller!"

"Two dollars and a half, two dollars and a half, going once, going twice, going, going, gone! Sold to young Matthew Miller!" the preacher exclaimed excitedly.

"Matthew Miller!" Clara choked in disbelief.

She saw José coming toward her as she stood petrified from the shock that she had to eat lunch with Matthew. She didn't want to spend one minute with that big dope, let alone a whole hour!

"Well, señorita, I tried to spend lunch with you. I had thought it a good time to go over some last minute things I remembered about the mountains. I'm sorry. I bid all my money and it wasn't enough. I think this boy really likes you. Has he been courting you?"

"Pew! Yuk!" Clara said, rolling up her eyes and wrinkling her nose. "He is just a big idiot who is driving me mad," she said.

"Will you be okay, señorita?" José asked concerned.

"I'll be fine, José. Can we get together another time?" she asked.

"Soon," he answered and walked away, as Matthew approached them.

"So little Clara Browning you packed lunch for me today. So sweet of you, my dear," he smirked, laughing into her face.

"Get out of here you big rat!" she yelled, turning her back toward him.

"Oh come on, Dear. Let's not have a little fit in front of these kind people," he teased.

"Matthew Miller you're one of the biggest bullies in Texas. You just eat that lunch that you stupidly wasted your money on all by yourself. I'll not spend one single minute with the likes of you," she stammered, walking away from him.

"Well, little missy, if you want to hear the message from your father, you better turn around and join me and behave like a lady. That is, if you know how!" he called out to her.

"Father? What about my father?" she asked, rushing toward him.

"In due time, Clara, in due time. Now, let's go sit by the creek and act like civil folks," he demanded in a cocky tone.

"You know I really do hate you, Matthew Miller," she seethed.

"The feeling is mutual," he answered loudly.

They sat down next to the creek and unwrapped the lunch contents. Matthew, surprised to see his mother's familiar cloths wrapped around the sandwiches and cookies asked, "Who packed this lunch you or my mother?"

"Your mother did. She, being a lady, and much kinder than the likes of you, shows thoughtfulness toward others," Clara sang out.

"Well the next time you are stupid enough to get yourself run over by a horse don't look for me to come carry you away. If I had been there, I would have left you lying in the street. Maybe a good stampede over the top of that thick skull of yours would knock some sense into you," he challenged.

"Oh, grow up, Matthew! You didn't rescue me. I got myself out of the fix. I didn't need the help of some big-headed farm boy. Not then, not now, not ever!" she rebuked.

"Are you forgetting that this farm boy carries a message for you?" he asked taunting her.

"Come on, Matthew, tell me where my father is and what he said," she asked more gently.

"Oh all right. The sooner I tell you the sooner this confounded lunch can end," he agreed.

After relaying Clara's father's message to her, Matthew threw his napkin down and walked away abruptly. Clara, left on the grass alone, looked deep in the shallow clear green creek. She surveyed the many deposits that the current brought with it. Small, pink shale stones and purple marblized pebbles adorned the roots of the tree that encroached into the creek bed. The rippling sound of the water flowing over the roots soothed her anger. Minnows nipped leisurely at the creek's bottom. The green watercress suddenly became a safe haven for the minnows to hide when larger fish came searching for food.

"Clara, Clara," a voice called from behind.

"Miss Simpson, what is it?" she asked.

"It's time for the games to begin. Come join us," she answered.

"I'm not feeling up to it, Miss Simpson. I need to go home and rest," she replied.

"Very well, my dear. Do take care," she said, strolling slowly away.

A tingling, burning sensation filled her numb legs as she stood up. Her back resisted the movement and cracked with the groan of an old woman. She slowly walked home. She thought of her father and the danger of being a sheriff. Her thoughts of her father brought thoughts of her mother. How she missed her. She didn't speak her mind, though, as she didn't want to open her father's wounds. It had taken him a long time to forgive himself for not being there when she died after giving birth to Jake. Just like now, he and a posse had fled to the mountains chasing bandits that day. His presence at the delivery would not have made a difference. Yet he somehow blamed himself for her passing. At first, Clara had blamed Jake. Several weeks had passed before she looked at him. Grandmother Browning had come from San Antonio and spent a year with them. With time, Clara had learned to love Jake. Her grandmother had helped her understand that the birth of one is not the cause of the death of another. Life cycled around the sun, stars, and moon that were all part of God's universe. Clara had struggled often with the God idea. "Who was he? Did he exist?" she wondered while walking home that bright afternoon four days before the race. The answers to her questions hid in the mountains eagerly awaiting her.

Chapter 18
Final Preparations

Clara organized her saddlebags in alphabetical order. A secret she had learned from Mrs. Miller. If she needed something quickly, its extraction, without her looking, came guaranteed. The food supply scarcely filled one side of the bags. Jerky represented the main staple. José told her berries would be plentiful. He had drawn her a map of the area and circled those places where she would find berries and fresh water. She had questioned his knowledge of the mountains. He had explained to her that he and his family came through the mountains when they left Mexico. They had spent several months traveling with a large band of people in the area the racecourse covered.

With the race being less than twenty-four hours away, Clara's thoughts turned toward the actual plot to enter the race today. She went outside dressed in a pair of pants and a shirt of José's. The past few days she had worked in the sun without any covering on her face and arms. Her skin glowed, golden bronze. The sun had bleached her hair enough that blond streaks bolted forward and mingled with the iron red hair shafts.

Her plan had worked out even better than she expected with her father still out of town. Flash and Clara had spent many hours practicing the pacing and steadying his heart rate. She had ridden in the breeches many times until they felt as if they were part of her skin. They allowed air to filter through the weaving. At first she seemed to slide in the saddle with the material's smoother surface. Eventually, she had learned the secret was to move up and down with Flash's movements instead of trying to stay steady in the saddle. Her body had ached and it pleaded with her to stop the training, but she pushed forward knowing the importance of being prepared.

She walked toward town, but turned off and went in from a different direction. The man taking race entries came from the mine, so he didn't know any of the local folks. Pulling José's sombrero snugly over her hair pulled and pinned inside, she staggered like a boy toward the entry table. Standing in line, many people she knew passed by. None of them seemed to look at her. When she reached the table, the man held out his hand saying, "Entry fee five dollars."

She handed him the money from her gloved hand and stood slumping over the edge of the table. His tobacco rich breath demanded erectness, though, so she stood up straight. "Name, horse's name, town of residence and next of kin," he asked hoarsely.

She gave him José's name and Flash The Sungiver for the horse's name. She told the truth when she said El Paso for residence and lied on the next of kin question. The man wrote the information down as one dauntless word followed the next from her deceitful lips. She kept her voice quiet and baritone. He looked up at her handing the entry form to her for a signature. She signed it so sloppy that no letter of the alphabet was recognizable. He pushed her entry number across the table at her and bellowed, "Next!"

She quickly moved toward home along an unfamiliar path to avoid being recognized. Once inside, she removed José's clothes and continued with her packing. With the packing completed, she went to the barn and cleaned Flash's tack thoroughly. She picked up the large boar bristle brush and began going over Flash's milk foam hair. Allowing her hand to glide slowly over almost one single hair at a time, she made him shine like the newborn moon. Flash responded eagerly to the attention and pushed his nose under her arm. With her arm hooked over his nose, she bent her head slightly and kissed her best friend. He snorted softly and blew out a long lip vibrating sigh.

Clara turned back to her task and continued brushing him. She lifted his mane and brushed tenderly along his neck. Hairs of the brush smoothly passed over the beauty mark that continued to haunt her. Forcing her eyes to focus on the mark, Clara stared at it until her eyes watered and it fell into a blur. "Where have I seen it before?" she cried. The rugged cliffs, perilous and silent, guarded the secret all these years, but would soon reveal the truth to her.

Chapter 19
"On Your Mark"

Courageously, Clara rode Flash through town disguised as José. She felt confident there wouldn't be a person in town to recognize José. Standing in the position given her, Clara anxiously waited for the starting pistol to go off. The judge walked around each rider and horse and verified their number. He climbed onto a platform in the street. After he finished calling out the rules of the race, he lifted the pistol and yelled, "On your mark, get ready, set, go!" "Crracckk" went the pistol in his hand. Clara and Flash pushed forward with riders and horses in front of them, behind them, and on both sides of them. The congestion broke up shortly after leaving the town's limits.

Hooves hit the ground with varying speeds and degrees of depression. Riders thrashed their arms and whooped and hollered with confidence. Many rode recklessly daring their challengers as they forged into the great adventure. Clara paced Flash at the slow gallop that caused her to bounce softly with his rhythm. Rhythmically she moved with his outstretched legs as they punched the hard, dry earth. Ticking melodically like a clock, she balanced herself and found her comfortable beat.

The first few hours slipped by uneventfully until she saw Matthew Miller. He rode toward her making her feel sick in her gut. She didn't know what he might do if he recognized her. Still in

105

José's clothing, Clara hoped he wouldn't probe too much.

"José, I see Clara chickened out. I figured she was yellow-bellied like her pa," he said riding up to her.

Clara was steaming mad. She had a mind to stop, turn around, and shoot him. Every encounter with him made her hate him even more. Finally she nodded her covered head acknowledging him and looked down toward the saddle horn.

"What do you say we set up camp together tonight?" Matthew asked.

"No thank you," Clara answered with a cough.

"Have it your way. You know Clara's not worth all the time you put into training her. But, now, that horse, well, I'd say he is a darn good piece of flesh. It's too bad he won't be much of a challenge for old Raven here," he said, racing off in front of Clara.

"Stupid boy!" she seethed between her clamped teeth.

With noon approaching, Clara decided to stop for a bite to eat and cool Flash off. She stayed out of the race for a good hour allowing Matthew to get far ahead of her. Before she climbed back into the saddle, she pulled off José's clothes revealing her riding breeches that were underneath them. She rolled the sombrero and clothes inside her sleeping roll and replaced it with her own hat. She kept her hair pulled up, though. She looked out at the scabby mountains that swelled upward in a coarse bulge and wondered how long it would take her to reach them.

By nightfall she and Flash reached the base of Mt. Franklin and began their ascent. Reaching a flat plateau, Clara gazed forward expecting to see the landmark José had described to her. She shifted her gaze farther to the east where the moon announced its arrival with brilliance. Casting its slender spiraled shadows of light in her direction, she noticed the tall tower shaped rock that José had spoken of. She walked forward with Flash's reins in her hand. He followed obediently. She walked downward following the ledge, keeping the tall projection in her sight.

Suddenly, an outburst of water rushing somewhere below her filled the canyon. The night's crisp, clear air magnified the eruption and exploded it into great resounding spouts. Following the waterway orchestra, Clara reached the river's embankment. Gently, she reached up and rubbed Flash's nose and said, "We made it to our first campsite." Flash thrashed his front hoof into the soaked ground along the river's bank. Clara listened to his request and unsaddled him quickly and turned him lose to drink and graze.

She gathered some dry wood and started a fire. Pete had taught her early on how to make a good camping fire. The burning wood snapped with its wild tongue licking up the air for rapid combustion. It roared as it consumed the air and digested it into its fiery, formless body. It projected a colorful illusion of blues and reds in various shades from powder to navy and light to blood.

Clara became so engulfed in the flame's performance, she didn't notice the dark figure standing on the opposite side of the river.

Chapter 20
River Stranger

An owl screeching caused her to look up.
She looked into the darkness of the basin and felt
completely isolated. The moon hung near the earth
almost touching the mountain peaks. Its silver
chord capturing ice crystals in the air sent forth a
teeth-chattering chill. The blaze of stars stood
silently watching her along with the mysterious
form that stood a riverbed away from her.

She turned her gaze across the river when
she heard a branch snapping. The figure, concealed
in the shrubbery growing along side the steady
stream, watched Clara as she rose to her feet
looking more closely at her surroundings. Steam
rose from the surface of the water as the cold air
greeted the sun-warmed waters of the day. Clara
reached her hand into the water and cupped a drink.
The snow-like freshness teased her tongue. Her
fingers left a morning dew fragrance on her face.
She wandered back toward the fire.

She realized that she had heard only
snapping, burning wood. It was silly to be afraid.
She separated herself from all the other riders by
following José's map. The other contestants had
navigated today by following the previous route.
This hollow was completely private and she shared
it with no other human being.

Exhausted and confident, Clara rolled out
her bedding and lay down. The night sounds lulled
her to sleep. The shrouded form moved quietly

downstream to a familiar crossing. Each step taken was precise and definite in purpose. Reaching the side of the river where Clara slept, the body of the stranger filled with an urgent feeling of confusion and questions. What was she doing here? How did she get here? The answers didn't matter. All that mattered was she lay here sleeping where she shouldn't.

She didn't belong. The clouds agreed, drifting frightfully overhead. Shadows danced briefly on her face when the clouds passed over greeting the dim light of the dying fire. She would not live through the night here in this gorge where she did not belong. At the slightest wrong movement, her life could end in an instant. She would not suffer. The cliffs would stifle her cries. The vultures feeding on her tomorrow would find little satisfaction in such a small meal. If she were buried along side the river, the bear with his big paws would dig up the grave. Like berries in a bowl, he would scoop her out and suck the marrow from her bones before disposing of them in a heap. Her life and death balanced effortlessly while she lay there sleeping. The figure controlled each breath that she took. The spontaneous inhaling and exhaling of breath may evaporate suddenly.

The stranger looked into the rushing water for guidance. It didn't make a difference to the gorge figure if she lived or died, or did it? The value of life meant little in these mountains. Survival captured all the authority out here. Death of intruders to survive and protect what was yours became a way of life in this territory. Silently the stranger dropped more wood into the eroding fire. Flames lashed outward demanding attention. It slowly hypnotized the form. Drawn into the sporadic behavior of the performing flames, the stranger didn't notice the movement from behind.

The nuzzle of the horse alarmed the being. After recovering from the fright, the stranger evaluated the value of a horse. Horses brought companionship and freedom. Those things that the stranger didn't have. Was her life worth the gain the darkened silhouette sitting by the fire would enjoy? She didn't belong. Her passing through here posed a threat to this private home. Her death meant no more to the traveler than her life. Horses belonged to the survivor of any battle. Even though the battle promised to be silent, the spoiled goods still became the victor's prize.

The lifting of the mane revealed the promised sign the stranger had waited for all these years. The same shape of the carved green stone that had hung from a leather strand that the river stranger had placed around the neck of a young white woman. She had hair that matched the tail of the red tail hawk. He had tied the strand around her slender neck before he had carried her to the town of many buildings. Many seasons had passed since then. Sitting next to the fire feeding it, the unknown person protected another red haired woman from those dangers that waited in the darkness. As dawn drew near and slits of light filtered into the concealed canyon, the stranger slid away silently into the brush across the river. If one looked hard enough, the eyes of the veiled protector of the night gazed over the rapid river watching until the sun rose. Those eyes promised a continuous journey following the girl that rode the flawless cloud covered horse.

Chapter 21
The Deadly Crossing

In a thin blanket of fog, Clara rose from her night's rest. She surveyed her surroundings quickly in the muted daylight. It appeared as José had said. The trees grew tall with long thick leafy boughs gracefully reaching down and sweeping the earth. Shrubs stood so thick together along the river, she found it impossible to tell where one ended and the next began. The river ran rapidly down a winding course. Its width stood about three wagons wide. According to José's map, Clara and Flash needed to cross the river to continue the race.

With cold water from the river, Clara filled the metal coffee pot. She dumped a scoop of coffee grounds into it and set it on the hot coals alongside the fire. Soon the crisp morning air captured the bursting, powerful aroma of black coffee. Clara sat down to a biscuit and jerky breakfast. She washed the hardened dough down with strong, bitter coffee. Coffee grounds floated down her throat with the flow of the hot, black liquid. She felt some grounds gather between the small gap between her front lower teeth. After she finished eating, she used the full length of her index finger to wash the food and coffee particles from her teeth. The river water's coldness made her teeth ache briefly as she rinsed them clean.

Flash wandered all around the area freely grazing on the tall, abundant, wide bladed riverside grass. He didn't reveal the visit from the stranger to

Clara in his behavior. She strolled down alongside the river to find a safe crossing. The water ran swiftly promising danger to the careless rider. The center of the river offered no bottom. The drop-off from the side came within a short distance of the embankment. This concerned Clara. She demanded of herself that she find a sure footed crossing. Down stream about a mile, Clara found a crossing formed by large rocks. The rocks looked large enough for Flash to walk on. With the crossing found, she headed toward camp to gather her belongings.

After Clara had broken camp, she saddled Flash. They slowly walked alongside the shore toward the crossing. Clara, leading Flash, stepped onto the first large, flat, gray rock that projected out of the swirling hissing foamy water. Flash yanked back on the reins and buried his feet deeply into the soft, moist ground and refused to follow her.

"Come on Flash. It's okay boy," she cooed while pulling harder on his rein.

Flash lifted his head straight up into the air and with wild, wide open eyes he snorted and pulled her off balance. Suddenly, Clara was thrashing outward with her arms in the chilled water. She grabbed for the rock, but is was too late. The swift undertow of the current sucked her under and carried her downstream at a fast pace. Her head bobbed up and she spat water and screamed for Flash to help her. Under she went again. Water filled her mouth and nose. Hot threads of water burned her nostrils. She threw her arms forward and kicked her feet and brought her head above the water's surface again.

Flash raced along the shore following her screams. Small heaps of rocks bruised and cut her body as she slammed against them in the raging river. Fallen limbs became blunt weapons smashing her head as the river plunged her forward. Her blood ran freely in the water. Clara, horrified, felt her exhausted body weight pull her toward the bed of the river. She slipped under the water again. Air bubbles rising from her obstructed her view. Her hair wrapped around her neck and face. Clara's lifeless form bumped along from one slimy, purple green moss covered rock to the next.

In a weakened state of mind and body, Clara managed to bring her head above water for the last time. She regained her thinking power and told herself not to panic. She forced her beaten body against the current and slowly turned herself over onto her back. She floated downstream at a high rate of speed. Clara's position blinded her, so that she could not see what dangers lay ahead of her in the river. The clouds danced gaily overhead on the blue dance floor of the open sky. Extending outward toward the opposite bank, trees full with new summer growth formed a canopy above her. Birds filled the trees above her and sang their morning songs. Squirrels chattered loudly as they ran up and down the trees' vine covered trunks.

The sun, now awakened by all the confusion, shared small slivers of brightness through cracks in the canopy. Clara knew she couldn't escape the death trap of this river. She

thought of her father and brother. Her father would
be angry. Clara feared he would blame himself,
because he wasn't home to stop her from entering
the race. Jake would feel the same emptiness she
felt when her mother died. Clara mothered him all
these years the best she could.

Suddenly the face of her mother appeared in
the now open sky above her. Her beautiful red hair
washed with blond streaks flowed beautifully
around her oval face. Her emerald green eyes
outshone the sun itself. Her smiling thin, pink lips
sang Clara a lullaby. The melody of the song
soothed Clara's body. She relaxed and stopped
fighting the battle with the river. The raging waters
carried her toward her mother. Clara waited,
anticipating the warmth that her mother's arms
would give her. Gathered in her mother's arms, she
knew she would be safe. Suddenly, Clara's head
exploded and darkness engulfed her.

Caught up in a stardust, breathless feeling,
she felt her mother's arms lift her upward. The
feather lightness of her head matched that of her
body. As a cloud, she light-headedly drifted to a
peaceful place. Clara moved her lips, but nothing
came out. She opened her eyes, but nothing
appeared. Water splashing and birds singing filled
her ears. Her body felt a warming all over it. She
knew she had entered Heaven. In her mother's
arms, she experienced the cradling of a baby.

Wrapped tightly in her bed roll next to a
roaring fire, she awoke with the high noon sun
overhead. "A dream! Just a dream," she thought.
But the moment she tried to move, she knew it

hadn't been a dream. The river still rushed loudly beside her.

"Flash," she called out weakly.

He came to her instantly and nuzzled her. He snorted and whinnied a loud greeting. Clara reached forward to touch his nose. His fresh, grassy breath filled her nostrils. She reached upward for her head and felt the dressing wrapped around it. Slowly Clara pulled herself to a sitting position. Carefully she surveyed the damage. Her arms, cut and scraped, had a thin layer of shiny ointment on them. Her legs, naked inside the bedroll, were slightly bruised, but not too badly. The aching in her back and hips revealed the true damage of her river adventure.

With her head throbbing like a tightly wound clock, she stood up. Feeling weak- kneed and dizzy, she sat back down. Slowly it came to her, somebody had fished her out of the river and had attended to her wounds. This same person had wrapped her in her bedroll and had built a fire to warm her. Looking toward the fire, she noticed a small clay pot sitting along the edge of the fire on some hot rocks. Crawling slowly toward it, she smelled a familiar odor. "Chicken broth out here, but how could that be"? she said aloud.

Feeling the hunger surging inside her, she pulled the pot toward her. After it cooled long enough, she lifted it to her lips and drank deeply. It tasted a little stronger than any chicken broth she had had before, but if definitely had the fowl taste. She drank it until gone. Feeling much better, she stood up and the dizziness she had experienced earlier disappeared.

Looking all around her, Clara tried to spy the person that saved her life. She saw no trace of any other. The sun moved in a westward direction signaling her that the day was wasting. Moving slowly, she rolled her bed and put it on Flash, still saddled and packed with all of her belongings. Taking a large stick, she walked to the river. In the soft, moist riverbank dirt, she wrote "Thank You."

Not until she mounted Flash did she realize that they were on the opposite side of the river. The side she had tried to reach this morning. It all seemed so very strange to Clara. First she fell into the river trying to reach the other side. Instead of being in Heaven, she woke up on the side of the river she had tried to reach on her own. Who had helped her? She assumed from what José had said that the gorge was so remote that most travelers wouldn't find it. But yet she knew, some other person had traveled through here and had saved her life. She shook off the eerie feeling it gave her and nudged Flash toward her unknown benefactor.

Chapter 22
Making Up Lost Time

Clara pushed Flash hard the rest of the day. They rode at a faster pace than they had yesterday. Following the river upstream as José instructed, she felt confident the terrain was safe to gallop faster than they had originally decided. Flash showed no signs of exhaustion. His feet plopped up and down digging deeply into the soft, wet earth. His hoof impressions filled quickly with water as he lifted his feet and moved forward. Often he had tried to break into a run, but Clara held him back.

With the sun setting and the daylight escaping much sooner than Clara hoped for, she finally allowed Flash to run against the speed of the wind. She tried to move with him to avoid the pain streaking through her body. Her spine smashed deep into the saddle with every footfall. Yet, she didn't slow him.

She rode into nightfall without taking a break. The moon shone brightly casting streams of light guiding the way along the river. With the night air came a coolness that made her shiver. She brought Flash to a walk. Reaching behind her, she untied the bed roll and wrapped the blanket around her shoulders. For several more hours they walked along the river. Clara, determined to find the next landmark, stayed in the saddle until the early morning hours.

Catching herself nodding into sleep, Clara began to hum. Her body felt as rugged as the cliffs appeared. Her hair, tattered from the wind, hung in large clumps of snarls. Her back worked its pain into a dull numbness. The darkness relieved the headache that the sun magnified. She preferred crying rather than humming, but knew that was useless. "Besides, only babies cry," she hissed to herself.

The river wound around Mt. Franklin, slowly winding toward the check-point. There a hot meal waited for the contestants, if they desired. Humming and looking ahead, Clara finally spotted the landmark José had spoken of where she was to turn away from the river. A huge knob protruding from the cliff above her hung like a rooftop. Stalactites hanging from it formed ghostly shadows on the deserted ground Flash now stood on.

Clara slowly climbed down from the saddle. Her legs felt like soft butter when she planted her feet on the ground. She held onto the saddle horn until she felt her legs strengthen. She pulled the saddlebags off first and then the saddle and other supplies. Pulling the bit from Flash's mouth, she sent him toward the river to graze. She looked at the protrusion above her and decided it made her feel too nervous to sleep under it.

Stumbling slowly about, she found some dry wood for starting a fire. Once she got the fire burning, she pulled the coffee pot out to brew something hot to drink. She hated the taste of the bitter choke-cherry flavored stuff, but it warmed her insides. She chewed on the hard, salty jerky she had packed and felt the juices hit the bottom of her empty stomach. With hot coffee in one hand and jerky in the other, Clara looked out at the somber night. Only a few stars dotted the black sky. Off in a distance, coyotes howled and yipped. It gave her no comfort to hear them. The yipping alarmed more coyotes to join the haunting choir, frightening Clara.

She added more wood to the fire to keep any coyotes away that may wander in her direction. With the moon lowering toward the west, she knew that daylight was only a few hours away. Her bedroll felt warm when she climbed into it. She lay just outside the edge of the natural roof above.

On the roof above Clara, the stranger lay belly down. She lay in clear view, so that he watched all of her movements. She moved stiffly about, enough so, that the stranger sensed her pain deep within himself. He had done all that he could to dress her wounds after he had pulled her from the river.

At first, he had thought her dead. When he reached her, her head, smashed against the tree that blocked the river, was soaked in blood. She didn't move when he picked her up. She lay limp in his arms while he carried her to the other side. Using the tree for a bridge, the horse had followed them to his side of the river. He had tried to get to her before she got washed too far down stream, but the water raced too fast in front of him. He had run silently with bare feet along one side while the horse stomped loudly, following her on the other. Their eyes met long enough for the stranger to reassure the beast that he, too, wanted to save her.

Carrying her to an open area, he had laid her down. Her weak pulse in her neck gave him hope that she may survive. Her body was frigid like the blocks of ice formed in the river during winter. Her blue gray lips and skin warned him that her internal temperature had fallen too low for survival. He unclothed her and wrapped her in blankets from the horse. Quickly he gathered wood and built a fire next to her. She didn't move as he had rubbed her hands and feet frantically. Once he had warmed her the best he could, he set out to gather berries, herbs, and fish oil to make an ointment to put on her wounds.

He wrapped her head with cloth that he tore from a shirt in her saddle bag. He fed the fire, just as he had the night before. The spirits, pleased with the stranger, had given him a sign. When he lifted her bleeding head, her blood mixed with his from an open wound he had suffered chasing her through the briar. The spirits filled his heart. Now this strange child had become his pup blood sister. He called to the sun and asked her name. The sun danced on his coal black long hair and called her name into the wind "River Turtle."

"River," called the Hawk, "whence she came."

"Turtle," cried the Eagle, "symbolizing Earth Mother with goddess energy, who cautions us of the jeopardy of challenging the river."

The stranger had streaked her nose with black mesquite bush oil and smudged his thumb prints on her cheek bones with the same oil to consummate the naming of the red haired child.

The turtle says, "Take your time. The fruit harvested too soon does not mature, leaving many to hunger. The same fruit, given time to develop fully, in its own season, will fill the bellies of all," the stranger sang in his native tongue while marking her.

The wind rustled among the trees this message for the stranger, "River Turtle has much growing to do. She cannot go home to the spirits yet. It is before her season. There are many who will prosper from her fruits."

He had sat beside her feeding the fire until she began to regain consciousness. Not wanting her to discover him, he had slipped into hiding and watched her. With his swift feet and knowledge of her destination that she had spoken of during her unconscious state, he managed to arrive at this very knob where he lay now at the same time she did.

Watching her now, she seemed to settle down quickly and fall asleep. The spirits charged him with the responsibility of protecting his pup sister. Another sleepless night lay ahead of him. After the raiding of his village many seasons ago, he had grown accustomed to sleepless nights and days. Most of his tribe had been massacred and the remainder captured while he lived in the woods on a vision quest. He had waited sixteen full summers to become a warrior. But he had returned a warrior to a vanished tribe. After offering the remains of his people to the spirits and tearing down all the *wickiups,* he had fled higher into these mountains. Many seasons had passed since then. He had become a friend to no person. He shared time with the animals Great Spirit had sent him. His education had come from those very creatures. They taught him through their habits. Many times through the years he had called upon his animal friends' power to ask for guidance and strength. They had never let him down, always sharing their wisdom with him.

River Turtle had the ability to call upon animal medicine for such power. However, she did not know that yet. In time, those powers the Spirits would reveal to her. For now, her guidance and strength came from within her. Earth Mother's abundant assistance lying deep within her had proved thus far to be all that she needed. The stranger, not given his warrior name, had developed into the external force River Turtle needed to guide her until the wisdom of the animal kingdom revealed itself to her. While she slept, he watched. No harm came her way this night, but it lurked, waiting for her higher in the mountains.

Chapter 23
Face to Face

Clara woke with a shiver. The early damp air had made her blanket heavy with moisture. The sun stalled below the surface of the earth. Flash grazed close enough for her to see him. She called out to him. He slowly walked with his head down toward her.

Clara wasted no time breaking camp. Deciding not to spend time building a fire, she moved quickly to warm herself. According to José's map, the check point wasn't much more than a few hours' ride. Clara slipped into José's clothing to avoid trouble when she reached the point.

Lifting her leg to the stirrup, she felt the heavy weight in her leg. Although the pain felt as if her veins would explode, Clara continued lifting herself into the saddle. She swung her other sore leg over Flash's wide muscular body and balanced herself in the seat.

Slowly she turned Flash away from the river and worked herself along the edge of the knob. The cliffs on both sides of her formed a narrow path. It seemed just wide enough for one horse and rider. She avoided looking straight up. Instead, she concentrated on watching the ground in front of her and guiding Flash cautiously upward.

Cactus jutted outward from the tall walls around her. Small, naked hedges clung to the granite boulders. The wind groaned above them sending sprays of chilling air downward. Sand swirled around Flash's feet with the movement of the air.

Clara concentrated hard on the path beneath their feet. She didn't notice the stray, bulging cactus hanging on the ledge beside her. Suddenly, Flash reared straight up on his back feet. Clara leaned forward and grabbed a handful of his mane. She felt the saddle horn dig deep into her stomach. "Easy Boy! Easy Boy!" she yelled, frightened.

Rocks under Flash's thundering feet rolled down the path behind them. Flash forged ahead and landed so hard on his front feet that Clara lost her breath when the saddle horn plunged and smashed into her navel. The pain sent vomit rushing up from her stomach. It burned a hot trail through her throat and shot out like a rocket when she opened her mouth.

Catching her breath and clamping her mouth shut, Clara sat up straight in the saddle. Fear ripped at her heart with a strangling hold. Salty tears fell down her cheeks and stung her scrapes as they washed over them. Her nose began dripping. "Stop this, Clara, right now!" she scolded herself.

She wiped her face with her sleeve. Clara didn't notice the black, oily smudge left on it. Cooing softly, she soothed Flash with a gentle stroking on his neck. She looked about the narrow passage and saw the cactus clinging to the clay-baked surface. Instantly, she knew Flash's behavior came from being poked with a thorn.

She unfastened the saddlebag and reached in without looking. Clara guided her finger tips over the contents. Following them from back to front, she located the cloth and salve, which she'd placed in alphabetical order. Clara wiped her nose and sucked in her last sniffle.

After shaking herself free of fear, she slowly pulled her right foot from the stirrup and brought her leg over Flash's rump. She shifted her body to the left and got out of the saddle. The cliff wall was tight against her as she settled her feet on the ground.

Not having enough room to walk around Flash, she stooped and walked under his belly. Gently she ran her hands and eyes over his body looking for the thorn. Flash nervously stomped his front feet. Hot, wet air frothed out of his nose as he snorted and looked frantically at Clara with his wide brown eyes. Clara sent her fingers rubbing and looking all over him.

She pressed her fingers tighter against his fur. "Ouch!" she yelled as the thorn stabbed her. Tiny drops of blood formed on the tip of her finger. With her forehead resting against Flash, she manipulated the thorn. She placed a thumb on each side of it and pushed inward toward the thorn. It popped out slightly as if the head of a pimple. She released the pressure and used her thumb and index finger like tweezers and tried to pull it out. It resisted and stayed buried in Flash's flank. Again, Clara pushed inward with her thumbs. The thorn moved outward enough for Clara to grasp it and pull it out. Flash immediately stopped fidgeting.

She opened the round salve tin and dipped her finger into it. With the tip of her finger, she smeared the thick, sticky substance over the small, but dangerous, wound. Clara looked up the path and judged they were about half way from the top. She crawled back under Flash and put the tin back in the saddlebag.

Pushing herself off the ground with one painful thrust, she slapped herself firmly into the saddle. Nudging Flash lightly, he moved forward. They walked deliberately, with great caution, the rest of the way through the narrow passage.

When they reached the ridge, she and Flash looked down at the rising sun. The sky, bathed in pink ripples of scattered clouds, held the sun hostage momentarily. Puffs of smoke floated slowly upward locating the check point for Clara. Her stomach ached from hunger and the punch it had taken earlier. She nudged Flash toward the rising smoke.

Based on the sun's position, Clara suspected it wasn't quite noon when she rode into the camp. Riders gathered around a wagon, eating. Clara dismounted and moved slowly toward them. She pulled the sombrero over her head as she got closer to them. A few of them looked up at her when she approached. She didn't recognize any of them. Clara sank the soup ladle deep into the black, cast iron pot and scooped out a bowl full of stew. She grabbed up two biscuits and walked toward the outer edge of the circle of men.

Sitting down on a log, Clara shoved an entire biscuit in her mouth. Her cheeks crammed full with dough made her face appear swollen with the bruises it sported. She gulped the food down and followed it immediately with a heaping spoonful of hot, spicy stew.

Wiping the bowl clean with the other wheat grain biscuit, she heard a familiar voice. Matthew, perched high on Raven, rode into the camp calling out to some of the others. He ambitiously jumped off Raven. His wide shoulders swiveled back and forth as he strutted like a rooster toward the food wagon. The entire time he smiled and talked in a loud, excited voice to the other men.

Clara turned her back toward him hoping to avoid an encounter with him.

"Hey, José!" he yelled toward her as he walked up behind Clara. She turned slightly to the side and nodded.

"I see you made it this far. They say the worst is yet to come. I haven't seen you. What trail you riding?" Matthew asked in a fast loud voice.

Clara gruffly said, "I followed the river." She got to her feet and started to move away from Matthew. Just as she was about to set a foot firmly on the ground, a rattlesnake slithered under it calling its threats into the air. Clara froze and Matthew cocked his pistol.

"Be real still, José," he whispered, bringing the gun up with outstretched arms and squeezing the trigger.

The snake flew into the air and its guts exploded all over Clara. She wanted to scream and run at the same time, but she didn't do either. Instead she nodded a thank you to Matthew and quickly moved toward Flash.

She led Flash away from the meeting place.
They walked through a grove of pine trees. Clara
saw a small pond at the edge of the grove. Its water
was stagnant. It gave off a moldy, swampy smell of
dead fish and frogs. The edges were crusty with
green algae.

Clara wanted to wash up, but she didn't have
the courage to put her hands into the disgusting
pond. She stepped out of José's pants and then
pulled the shirt up over her head. With her head
inside the shirt, she heard something moving in the
deep grass along the edge of the pond. She brought
the shirt slowly over the back of her head, down
over her face, and off her chin. Matthew stood
looking at her with his jaw gaping open.

"Clara Browning! What in tarnation are you
doing out here?" he demanded.

"What do you think I'm doing out here," she
answered sarcastically.

"You know darned well girls ain't supposed
to be in this race. Why, if I'd known that was you
back there, I'd let that snake go and bite you. You
best turn yourself around and head for home."

"I'll do no such thing. It is none of your
business who is in this race!" she yelled back at
him.

"I'm going to turn you in. They'll kick you
out, Little Missy," he hissed stomping away.

"Go ahead! But you know darned well, the
only reason you're turning me in is because you
know I'll win the race," she screamed throwing
José's shirt at him.

"What! You're crazy, Clara! Just like that pa of yours! There ain't no way you can beat Raven and me!"

"That's where you're mistaken, Farm Boy!" she spat at him.

"Farm Boys are better than little girls who think they are something they're not," he yelled back.

"Really! You think being a boy gives you special privileges, don't you?"

"Think!...It does! And you better start getting used to it. You are a girl, Clara, plain and simple, A GIRL!" he shouted close to her face.

"Really, Matthew, I didn't know that. Thanks for telling me, Your Majesty. Now get out of here!" she yelled back.

"I'm leaving and you're coming with me," he said grabbing for her.

She yanked away from him and spouted, "I'm going nowhere with you. Get lost!" She turned and ran toward Flash.

Suddenly, Matthew dashed toward her and tackled her from behind. She struggled and tried to free herself, but his size overpowered her. He wrapped his long, hard arms around her waist and pushed the backs of her knees with his. She tumbled to the ground hitting it with a heavy thud. He went down sprawling on top of her. Her body, so tiny compared to his, disappeared beneath him. Dirt filled her nose and grass blades surrounded her face, almost blocking off her air supply.

"Get off me you big hog," she muffled into the damp, musty ground.

"I said, you are coming with me. If I have to hog-tie you, I will," he seethed between clenched teeth.

"You have no right bossing me around. Let me up right this minute, or I'll scream!" she screeched.

"Go ahead and scream, Little Girl!" he laughed.

"Get off me! I can't breathe," she cried.

He rolled off her. Clara rolled over unto her back and then pulled herself up onto her butt.

"Clara," he said more calmly, "You can't stay in the race. It is too dangerous for a girl."

"Leave me alone," she said. "I can take care of myself."

"Take care of yourself. Just look at you. You're a filthy, tattered mess. And what's those black marks smudged all over your cheeks and nose for?"

Clara put her hand on her face and rubbed her finger across her cheek. She brought her finger into her view and looked at the black oil on her fingertip. She had no idea what it was, but she wouldn't let that overgrown farm boy know it.

"It's none of your business!" she said, looking Matthew straight in his blue eyes.

"Get up! You're coming with me!" he demanded, angry again.

Clara jumped up and moved quickly to the edge of the pond. Flash joined her. She reached up to the saddle horn and, with a single swift jump, she was in the saddle. She reeled Flash around and Matthew ran to her side. As he reached up to grab her, she kicked him in the ribs with her foot and sent him rolling into the pond.

He splashed about and yelled obscenities at her as she rode away. She pulled José's map from her pocket and unfolded it, holding the reins in her teeth. She let Flash run as fast as he wanted to. They needed to put as much space between them and Matthew as possible.

Clara needed to figure out as quickly as she could how to get to the trail drawn on the map. If she could accomplish that, Matthew wouldn't be able to find her. Dust and dirt kicked up behind them surrounding her and Flash in a thin veil of brown powder. The trees thinned and sagebrush tumbled about in the breeze their speed caused. One strange shaped cactus after another stood tall. They waved their limbs at her as she raced along their prickly path.

She looked for a group of five or six cacti that formed a church steeple. Clara needed to head north from them toward the turning point of the race. The longer she rode away from Matthew and his ugly words the more she hated him. Why did she always feel she had to prove herself to men? The only male that didn't make her feel that way was Pete. Pete represented the grandfather she had never known. He was as old and rugged as the mountains themselves, she figured. Even though he was hard and gruff, he had always treated her with kindness and patience. He had never separated her from the men when it came to doing. He said, "Whoever is here to do, will do. Those who ain't, won't!"

Pete had told Clara he expected her to work just as hard as the others on the range. He had made no special provisions for her because she was a girl. Clara worked just as hard as the men. She wrestled calves to the ground and held them down while he branded them. Sometimes the early born calves outweighed her, but she listened to Pete's instructions and dug her feet deep into the ground and used her upper body to hold them down. The twisting of their heads caused enough pain to force the calves to lie still long enough for the branding iron.

Her father, though, didn't think like Pete. He thought like most men. Girls aren't much and can't do much beyond women's stuff. She loved her father, but she hated his ignorant, narrow minded way of thinking when it came to her. She didn't think he felt she was incapable, but she couldn't do it, because God made her a woman. "And that's another thing," she hissed into the air, "Why did God have to make men so pig-headed and stupid. What was he thinking, anyway?"

The whole God issue bothered her often. Almost as often as the men's issue bothered her. "Rulers of the Universe!" she gasped and then began laughing when she thought of how pitiful Matthew had looked thrashing about in that smelly pond. She had conquered the big thug and beat him at his own game.

"I hate him. He is so self righteous," she thought. Twice now she had put him in his place. First she scared him with his own gun and now this. She hoped he felt as foolish as he was. Although

she had no way of knowing it, he was far from feeling foolish.

Chapter 24
The Murder

Matthew pulled himself out of the pond. He felt the anger boiling deep inside himself. Dripping like a submerged rag, he jumped on Raven and punched him with his spurs. Raven jumped into a fast run. Matthew figured Clara would keep heading on the race course. "Stupid Girl!" he yelled into the wind.

"When I catch her, I'm going to do something her father should have done a long time ago. I'm going to put her over my knee and spank her back side!"

Matthew kept Raven running at a fast pace. He didn't dare let up. He knew Flash was fast. He figured, by the looks of him, he was fresher than Raven. "Why?" he wondered. It made a difference. Flash, being fresher, would have an edge on Raven. Matthew became obsessed with winning the race. Clara couldn't get ahead of him. His entire future depended on Matthew's ability to win the race. Without the ranch he would have nothing. His mother was his responsibility. He knew he couldn't let her down.

He wondered again about the strange circumstances surrounding his father's murder. He had remembered much more than he let on to his mother. It had happened late one cold fall night. The wind groaned and whistled as it swept over the desert making the curtains on his bedroom window blow inward. The chilled air had wakened him. He sat up in his bed to pull the extra blanket over him when he heard a loud thud, thud, thud outside. He had crept out of bed and pulled his pants over his night shirt. He wrapped his buffalo skin blanket around him and quietly opened his door.

The fire in the fireplace had scattered dim, light sparks across the floor of the main room. Matthew had seen no one, so he moved across the floor to the door. When he stepped out on the porch, he saw the barn doors beating and swinging back and forth against the barn. The wind moved them as if they were paper dolls. The moon bathed the ground with shadowed light that disappeared momentarily as small black clouds passed over it.

As Matthew stepped off the porch, the step closest to the ground creaked under his young weight. He glanced over his shoulder at the house to see if he woke his parents. There was no movement inside, so he continued toward the barn.

The thudding had grown much louder and the wind had gusted, slamming them more savagely into the building. He reached for the door closest to him and pushed it shut with his entire body. Holding it firmly, he bolted shut the door. He had walked to the other door. As he reached upward for the door, he had heard voices coming from inside the barn. He crouched down against the ground to go unnoticed. The groaning wind and slamming noise had prevented him from making out what was being said. He couldn't be sure who was in there. He had sat there against the barn opening wondering if he should go inside the barn, or go to the house for his father.

"His father...Where was he? Matthew thought back to supper time. His father, drunk as usual, had argued with his mother during supper. Then he left. It could be his father inside the barn, but who would he be talking to?" Matthew wondered. He heard one of the speakers yell loudly, but its volume was muffled too much for him to know what had been said.

He had moved inside the barn to try to identify the speakers. Moving closely to the ground, he slid inside the first stall and hid in the shadows. The lantern burned a pumpkin orange fire near the speakers in the barn. The fire danced slowly inside the glass tube sending black smoke out its stack.

Matthew heard a rope rubbing against the wood above him. He looked up, but saw nothing. Yet the noise continued and intensified. The noise had a definite, constant swaying to it. The wind blew the unfastened door against the barn with a slamming force. Matthew jumped with the blast of wood against wood. As he jumped, he saw a shadow swaying against the barn beams further back toward the voices.

He couldn't make out what it was from the angle where he was hidden. He slowly crawled along the stall and moved closer to the rear of the barn. Matthew tipped his chin upward and lifted his eyes to the back of his head and had a sick stab in his gut at the sight that hung above him.

There, swaying in the shadows of the lantern, hung a man. A thick rope tied around his limp neck from a large rafter held him suspended in the air. Matthew had not been able to see who the man was, but he knew by the figure it wasn't a woman.

The voices grew louder. He finally made out the voice of his father, swearing and slurring his words as if his tongue were thick as a tree limb. The other voice seemed crisp and clear. Matthew didn't recognize the second speaker, though. He laid there listening to the conversation of his drunken father and the other man, but he still hadn't been able to make out every word being said. He crept closer. Just as he turned past the last stall, he heard groans and flesh being hit with flesh. Harnesses had gotten knocked over and pails had gone clamoring and flying. Matthew turned to run out the door when a gun fired. He had frozen in horror. "Father!" He cried. He rushed into the barn and there at the feet of that murdering sheriff laid his father, dead! From there it was a blur. Matthew shook himself free of the memory that haunted him often the past six years.

Raven continued running. Matthew still saw no sight of Clara. "There ain't no way I'm going to let that murderer's daughter beat me. No way! No way!" he yelled angrily into the scorching noonday.

Chapter 25
Steeple Chase

Finding the five cacti standing together that looked like a church steeple, Clara turned Flash north and left the main race course. She moved quickly upward, higher than the trail she had left. She wasted no time getting out of sight of the other riders. Flash pushed his legs against gravity as he climbed up the steep, rugged mountainside. Rocks and dirt cascaded behind them as they moved slowly along the side of the mountain.

It became so steep that Clara decided she should climb down and lead Flash the rest of the way up. With his reins in her hands, she cautiously half crawled up the steep embankment. When she finally reached the top of the first rise, she looked straight down into a canyon hundreds of feet deep. The ridge was almost wide enough for two riders to ride along side each other. José had said to follow the ridge for many miles. He had told her that there was a natural land bridge several miles up the ridge. Clara looked all around her. She felt as if she stood on top of the world. She stood looking down on top of the lower mountains. She marveled at the forests that lay hidden deep in the canyons. Thick cotton white clouds mushroomed around the mountain peaks disguising their savage ruggedness. To the west she looked across the endless desert. Its land lay dry and barren. Its repulsive creatures, the snakes and lizards, crawled, dragging their bellies along the hard parched earth. The tarantulas moved slowly along the sandy desert seeking insects and millipedes to eat. Their poor eye sight offered them no help in finding their food. However, their extreme delicate sense of touch finds everything in their domain. Clara shuddered at the thought of tarantulas. Her father had once told her that their sight is bad, but don't ever come down toward one. They can see the movement coming down on them and if they do they will rise on their hind legs, lift their front legs, and open their fangs to give a painful bite. "It won't kill you," he had said, "but it will hurt so bad you'll wish you were dead!"

Clara made herself stop thinking of the hideous things and moved toward the natural land bridge. The sun shone brightly against her back all day as they came up the mountainside. It had burned her skin through her shirt. Her head itched from the sweat that had built up inside her hat and soaked her hair. Her body odor seemed to her to be like a rotten piece of meat. She felt sick to her stomach each time she smelled herself. "Flash, do I look as terrible as I smell and feel?" she asked the horse that obediently followed her along the ridge.

Clara and Flash worked their way along the ridge for several miles. Clara's feet burned with blisters seeping hot moisture into her boots. Her socks, feeling as if made of sandpaper, rubbed against her skin. Each time she lifted her foot to move forward it felt as if it had picked up another rock in the sole. Her legs ached around her knees. They felt like brittle branches each time she bent them to take a step. Her upper body burned from the hot sun's baking. Her head pounded like a blacksmith's hammer pounding against red hot iron.

Clara had not crawled back into the saddle, because she felt uneasy about the ridge. She didn't want to take a chance of having Flash step off the edge. It appeared wide enough, but there were spots that it narrowed down to allow just one sure-footed horse to walk. The sun began descending in the west. It chiseled spurts of orange and pink shafts of light through the heavily clouded evening sky. Clara felt glad to see the clouds moving overhead. Perhaps a rain shower worked its way toward her. If not, at least the cloud cover would keep it a little warmer once the sun went down.

Clara stopped to get a drink. As she lifted her canteen, she saw the land bridge about a mile up ahead. She smiled and put the canteen back on the saddle and patted Flash. "We've made it Flash. Look! Just ahead! The bridge!" she said between half giggles and sobs.

She began running and Flash followed quickly behind her. They crossed over the land bridge and began slowly moving down the other side of the canyon. José had told her that there were small natural hot springs down inside the narrow tunnel that cut through the canyon wall. Her body begged to be in the hot springs. With that thought in mind, Clara moved swiftly causing the loose earth to tumble ahead of her and Flash.

Suddenly, she lost her footing and fell to the ground. She slid on her bottom with the dirt and small rocks rolling with her. She managed to let go of Flash's reins, but he followed closely behind her as if she were still leading him. She tried to stop herself, but couldn't fight the gravity. Her boots quickly filled up with dirt and pebbles. Her bottom felt like a pincushion. Her legs bumped along the rocky ride bouncing up and down like a kangaroo.

Finally, Clara's ride ended at the bottom of the canyon. She slowly pulled herself up and stood on her feet. Her boots felt like a bucket full of dirt, so she sat back down and pulled them off. She dumped the boot's contents onto the ground. She forced her swollen feet back into the boots and stood again. Picking up Flash's reins, she turned toward the setting sun and walked slowly looking for the tunnel. The tunnel would offer shelter for the night. She soon heard the sound of cascading waters. She continued walking toward the sounds of rushing water. As she turned a bend, she saw the massive waterfall that José had spoken of. It gushed spurting water all around it. The water ran so clearly that Clara could see its limestone bottom. It didn't appear rocky or rugged. She knew she was close to the tunnel now. José had said the waterfalls were just before the tunnel. She began looking to her left. He had said to look carefully, because wild grapevines covered its opening. The birds were chirping loudly as they gathered berries alongside the pool. Some snatched up insects and sat on the big stones eating and watching Clara. She saw a few birds fly to the canyon wall and land in some vines. They didn't pick the small, green grapes from the vine, but sat there momentarily chirping at each other. She looked closely and saw that curtains of vine covered the tunnel's opening.

"We've made it, Flash. We're here!" she cried and flung her sore, tired arms around Flash's thick neck. He snorted and bobbed his head up and down.

She unpacked Flash as quickly as she could. He wasted no time getting into the pool up to his knees and drinking. She watched him as he moved in deeper so that the water covered his back completely. He thrashed his head up and down snorting and whinnying. He then slowly walked out of the pool and dropped to the ground and rolled over onto his back several times. When he stood up, he shook his body so hard the ground trembled under him. Satisfied with his bath and roll, Clara watched him as he wandered around and found some small patches of grass to eat.

Happy that Flash was taken care of, Clara quickly set up camp. She decided to get the firewood gathered before it got too dark. She really wanted to soak in the hot springs inside, but knew she had to take care of business first. With the wood gathered, she went deeper into the tunnel toward the springs holding a candle she had brought with her. She knew she was close when she felt the temperature change. Suddenly, the air was very warm and moist. The candle flickered and cast its shadow on the tunnel's walls. The soft rippling of the water bubbled and overflowed along its edges.

Clara set the candle down and undressed quickly. She stuck her big toe in first to test the temperature. "Oh! This is much warmer than I ever expected," she said aloud. She put both feet in. Immediately the warm water swirled around her ankles and invited her to come in farther. Clara walked into the water slowly allowing each unsubmerged part of her body to enjoy the splendid warmth one piece at a time. Finally she had water all the way up to her chin. It felt like a hot bath on a cold, winter night. She walked around the pool of water letting her slowly moving muscles feel the warmth. Finally she found a large boulder that made a good seat along the spring's edge. She sat down and lifted her legs. The jetting water forced them upward and she balanced herself with her hands against the boulder.

The tunnel filled with the echo of running water. It was so relaxing and peaceful. It felt magnificent sitting in the hot water and relaxing for the first time in days. Clara confessed to the empty walls that she wished she didn't ever have to leave this place. After several minutes of sitting and relaxing on her granite chair, Clara plunged forward and went under the water. The water rushed through her hair. With her hair completely wet, Clara used her fingernails to scrub her scalp. It tingled as she dug deeply into it and massaged it with pressure. Then she placed her index fingers on her temples and rubbed in a circular motion to relieve her headache.

Droplets of water glistened on her red, bronzed skin. Clara decided while sitting in the pool that she would bring her bedroll back by the spring for tonight. It was warm enough without a fire. She could wash her clothes in the spring and hang them outside to dry. She knew she would be warm sleeping rolled up in her blankets without any clothes.

She reluctantly got out of the warm bath. She dunked her breeches, shirt, and underclothes into the water. She made a swirling motion and plunged them up and down against the boulder as if it were a scrub board. Satisfied that they were as clean as possible, Clara picked the candle up and walked back to the tunnel's opening. She stepped outside. The cool night air quickly made bumps rise on her skin. She unrolled her bedroll and wrapped the blanket around her thin, naked body. She had plenty of fresh water to drink with her jerky and biscuit dinner. After she hung her clothes on the vines nearby, she picked some mint leaves and bade Flash a good night and walked back into the tunnel. She carried her dinner with her in one hand and her candle and sulfur matches in the other.

She laid the blanket out on the tunnel's floor and sat there eating a light picnic dinner. She felt so satisfied. Her muscles didn't seem to ache as much. Her headache had disappeared. The warm, moist air made her feel safe and secure. After she ate, she rubbed the mint leaves she had picked earlier all over her body and especially under her arms. The tingling smell of fresh mint filled the air. It made her nose tickle. It reminded her of the peppermint candy that she loved to eat at Christmas, so she put an unused leaf in her mouth. It tasted just as good as the Christmas candy. She sat there chewing the leaf slowly and watching the shadows dance on the walls. It was a superb performance, she thought.

Clara felt herself drifting toward the gap which is the space that lies just between awake and asleep. The quiet, undisturbed place that you slip into before you are fully asleep and just before the dreams begin. The gap of discovery where you take your day's troubles and leave them. The place where futures get spun by the Universe. God's throne, where he wraps his arms around you and slowly rocks you to sleep.

The angels sprinkle stardust into your eyes and stir your imaginative dream maker. The dream maker takes the past and spins it with gold slivers of tomorrow and creates the dream the subconscious desired during the waking hours. Clara lay down with her tender skin against the softened wool blanket. She rolled herself in it like a cocoon, naked in the wrappings like the butterfly that awaits metamorphosis. The angels didn't ask the dream maker to spin her a dream with the true future in it. They wished her to sleep peacefully before her nakedness caused her certain deceitfulness in the morning.

Chapter 26
Naked Discovery

  Early the next morning as the birds began their songs, somebody crept silently outside the tunnel opening. He knew she was here. The horse grazed quietly. Flash made no sudden moves when he saw the figure approach. Her articles of clothing lay across the vines. Her gear and supplies lay in a heap on the ground. He wondered where she was so early in the morning with the campsite looking so strange. There didn't appear to be a fire ring anyplace.

  Suddenly, he heard somebody coming through the small stretch of trees. He hid himself behind the cascading waters. He could see through the falling waters the movement by her campsite. A man appeared with golden hair and a large black horse. The horse was as black as any bear he had ever seen. The man didn't appear to be enough seasons old to be the father of River Turtle. He hid, concerned that this man didn't belong here. He told the Great Spirit that he would watch quietly and do the needed to protect River Turtle from this intruder.

  Matthew looked around at Clara's makeshift campsite. He did not see any evidence of a camp fire. He saw her clothes stretched about for drying. Her saddle and supplies lay in a huge heap on the ground. "Where in tarnation has that girl made off to," he sputtered. He felt exhausted after tracking her up that darned mountainside. Where she had thought she was going, he couldn't figure out. But he wasn't going to let her pull any tricks and end up winning the race, so he had decided to follow her.

It had gotten too dark once he had reached the bottom of this side of the canyon to follow her, so he made camp for the night. He didn't sleep well. The whole night he had tossed and turned with one crazy dream after another. Where he had ever come up with such foolish notions to dream about was beyond him. "Gol-darned girl, anyway!" he seethed.

He decided that wherever she was, she would be returning. He filled her coffee pot with water from the pond and dug out her coffee grounds and put a handful in the pot. He made a fire with the wood Clara had gathered the night before. With coffee boiling on the fire, Matthew leaned back against her saddle and chewed on a piece of her jerky and listened to the waterfalls and birds while he tried to figure out the map he had found in Clara's saddlebag. Raven grazed next to Flash quietly on the lush green tufts of grass growing sparingly here and there.

Clara woke up feeling more refreshed than she had in some time. She felt as if the weight of the world had been lifted from her shoulders. All the lying and deceiving she had been doing in the past few weeks had weighed on her more than she knew. The warmth of her secret tunnel engulfed her. She lay there thinking of where José's map would take her today. She tried to remember the details of it, but she just couldn't. It didn't matter. The map was safe in her saddle bag with her food.

She planned to go over it while she ate breakfast this morning. She sat up trying to decide if she wanted to dip into the springs again, or if she should get some coffee brewing when she realized that she could smell coffee. She knew it was much more than the power of suggestion.

Alarmed, she jumped to her feet and wrapped the blanket around her. She grabbed the other few items she had brought in last night and headed toward the opening. She did not light the candle, as she didn't want to draw any attention to herself. She followed the smell of the coffee and walked closely against the tunnel wall until she could see just a few little slits of light coming through the dense vines draped over the opening.

She moved to the opening cautiously so as not to make any noise. She peeked out through the vines and saw Matthew sitting on the ground. "How in the world did that big fool ever find me?" she silently questioned herself.

What was she going to do? He sat out there with her clothes and everything else she currently owned. She knew he wasn't just stopping for a free breakfast. He had more than likely come to gather her up and take her to the race officials. Somehow she had to get him to cooperate with her long enough for her to escape from him again.

With no real formulated plan in mind she succumbed to the idea that she had to be nice to him if she wanted him to cooperate with her. Being nice to him placed a high demand on Clara. The last thing in the world she ever planned to do in her life was being nice to Matthew Miller. Once she had felt sorry for him, but never again. She just plain hated him now and wished him the rottenest of luck! "No sense standing here wishing the circumstances were different," she whispered to herself as she moved toward the opening.

"Good morning, Matthew," she said politely through the vine curtain.

Matthew darned near swallowed his cup when she spoke. He jumped up and looked all around for her. A little scared and confused he asked, "Is that you, Clara?"

"Well, of course it is me. Who did you expect?"

"Where in tarnation are you, you little sneak?"

That made her angry enough to pull a little sneaky trick on the big overgrown bully. "Well, Matthew, can't you see me? I'm sitting right here on the saddle sipping the coffee you made."

"Ugh, Clara, I don't see you on that saddle. You just quit playin' games with me and tell me where you really are!" Matthew demanded, shaking a little.

"Matthew Miller, what's gotten into you. Did you go blind or something? Don't you be funnin' with me. Now get on over here and pour me some more coffee," she replied.

"Clara, you are the one funnin' with me around here. Now, you just come out from wherever it is you're hiding, right now!"

"Oh! Dear, Matthew, I fell in the pond last night while I was bathing in the waterfall. I really

152

thought I hadn't drowned. But if you can't see me, then I guess I must have," she cried.

"Don't be ridiculous, Clara. You'd know if you were dead. Wouldn't you?"

"I always thought so, but now I'm not so sure. I'm sitting right here almost close enough to touch you, and you say you can't see me. What do you suppose that means, Matthew?"

"I suspect that it means one of us is crazy, or one of us is a liar!" he exclaimed.

The entire time the unnamed warrior had watched and listened, amused, from behind the waterfall. He felt tempted to add a little flavor of his own to the death melodrama, but decided that River Turtle was holding her own on the life and death stage. He remained quietly awaiting the next act.

"Oh, my! You'll have to tell my father of my unfortunate demise. I'll wait here until my soul is accepted either in Heaven or well you know..." she quietly said.

"Clara Browning, you ain't dead. If you were, you wouldn't be talking to me. Would you?" he asked, beginning to believe this situation could be true.

"Well, what am I supposed to know about being dead. I've never been dead before. I do know that I died naked, though. I don't want to enter through the pearly gates naked, so would you please hand my clothes over to me," she asked sweetly.

"Who cares how you are dressed when you get to Heaven, or well you know.... Besides if you go there, it'll be so hot you won't be needing your clothes anyway," he said, gathering up her clothes that hung about and threw them on the saddle where she was supposed to be.

"That's probably true, but I don't want to make a bad first impression either place. Would you be kind enough to hand them to me after I move, so I can get dressed without your watching me?"

"What in tarnation are you talking about, girl? I can't see you now. How am I going to be able to watch you get dressed?" he asked, disgustingly.

"Come on, Matthew, it is my last request. Who knows? Any second now I could evaporate into thin air, and you'll never hear from me again. That is, unless they let me haunt the person who didn't give me my last request," she said teasingly.

"Oh, for Heaven's sake where are you now, so I can hand you the clothes?" he said surrendering to the entire foolish idea.

"I'm standing inside the grapevines just in front of you. Poke them through the little opening on the left side. Thank you, Matthew. I always knew you had a kind heart," Clara said, moving back slowly and quietly into the tunnel's shadows.

"Yeah, a kind heart, all right!" he said, poking the clothes inside the vine opening and never looking deeply into the vines to discover the truth.

Clara quickly got dressed. She couldn't believe how her little game of deceit brought on by anger had actually worked. Half of her problem was solved with her clothes back on.

The unnamed warrior stood shaking his head. He laughed with Great Spirit over how well River Turtle's gentle wickedness had won the first battle. This little pup sister turned out to be much more clever than he had suspected. Perhaps they would learn from her, too. He had not figured out what she planned to do next. He didn't fully understand the relationship between her and the young man. He waited patiently, though, for act two. He again assured Great Spirit that he planned to intervene, if necessary, to protect River Turtle.

"Are you dressed now?" Matthew asked.

"Yes, thank you I am," Clara replied, walking out through the vines.

Matthew jumped at the sight of her. She looked lovely. Her skin was glowingly clean and her hair was shining, captured in the sun's rays. She smelled like mint. *"Boy, death did her justice,"* he thought.

Clara stood in front of the vines and smiled at Matthew who looked as if he had seen a ghost. "Matthew, are you all right?" she asked sweetly.

"I'm fine. It's just that I can see you now. You look just great, Clara. Too bad you didn't look that good when you were alive," he said smiling.

"Well, what do you think I am, DEAD?" she laughed, loudly.

"Nope, I never for a minute thought you were dead, Clara. Why if you were dead, the entire earth would be celebrating your passing into the unknown!" he shouted back at her.

"Oh, you liar, Matthew. I had you fooled and you know it," she scolded.

"Afraid not, Clara. I knew where you were the whole time. You were just too proud to ask me to hand you your clothes, so you had to make up your little death story. I should have held out and made you step outside that vine curtain naked. But, what the heck, I'm sure you ain't worth looking at, anyhow," he said cuttingly.

"Perhaps!" Clara stated while pouring some coffee into a tin cup.

"You know why I've come for you, don't you, Clara?"

"I guess it's my company you want to keep. Right, Matthew?"

"Very funny, Clara. I'm taking you to the race officials and turning you in for being an impostor. I expect you'll come along peacefully. Is that right?" he asked, with that cocky tone of his.

"Well, of course, Matthew. There's no reason for me to resist you anymore. You'll not leave me alone until you have done the proper thing, I suspect," Clara said, holding her wrists out toward him, "well, where are the handcuffs?"

"Don't be silly. I'm not going bring you in like a criminal. Your father would throw me in jail for treating his little angel badly."

"You can be sure of that," Clara agreed, chewing on some jerky.

The unnamed warrior watched as River Turtle and the young man broke camp and packed her horse. River Turtle behaved very casually. He knew that her softened behavior meant that she must have a plan for escaping this young captor.

156

He thought hard about what animal power had come to her. It had to be deer. The deer teaches gentleness. The power of gentleness will touch the hearts and minds of those trying to keep us from entering the Sacred Mountain. The Sacred Mountain is that which we desire most in a certain situation. River Turtle's Sacred Mountain was the goal of winning the race. Her captor tried to block her way. With love and kindness, both light and dark can be overcome to open the pathway to the Sacred Mountain. Yes, the unnamed warrior knew that Deer had gently nudged her way into River Turtle's being and was guiding her to freedom.

He quietly moved from behind the waterfall and began silently following the two. He had no idea where River Turtle planned to finish the battle with this young yellow haired man. He couldn't know the danger that they all walked toward. If he had known of the horrible danger waiting for River Turtle and her captor, he would have intervened back at the waterfall. But Great Spirit did not reveal the horrendous battle that lay before his pup sister. Many times, the unnamed warrior has asked Great Spirit why no warning was sent and never has Great Spirit revealed the reason.

Chapter 27
Wasps

Clara obediently followed Matthew through the thick brush and trees along the canyon wall. Wings flapped noisily in the sky above them as they walked under the trees where the birds perched. She had tried to carefully pay attention to the way they had gone since leaving the waterfall. Clara could see that Matthew looked straight ahead and studied the area with great concentration. While he appeared absorbed, Clara unfastened her saddlebag and reached in for her map. She began at the back and worked forward using the alphabetical procedure. However, she did not find it. She again ran her fingers through the saddlebag feeling for the map. Still it was not there. She pulled her foot out of the stirrup and lifted the saddlebag toward her. She looked deeply into it. The map did not appear to be in the bag. Perhaps, she had put it in the other side in haste yesterday. She unfastened the other side and lifted the saddlebag into view. The map wasn't in there, either. Clara thought hard trying to figure out when she last saw it. She knew it was on the ridge. She had put it back before leading Flash along the ridge toward the land bridge.

Just as she began rummaging through her saddle bag, Matthew turned his head around and looked at her over his broad shoulder. "What are you looking for?" he asked.

"Oh, nothing- well, I'm sort of hungry, so I thought I'd get some jerky. Would you like some?"

she asked, stammering with the quickly thought up lie.

"Nope, I don't want anything of yours, Clara Browning," he answered, rudely.

"Suit yourself," she answered, softly.

Clara tried to bring the map into her mind. As she concentrated, the map appeared in her head. She looked at it and found the waterfall. She concentrated on the route leading from the waterfall. She saw the flat, round slab rock that sat high on a thin towering pile of rocks. She remembered she had to turn south at that rock and head toward the Río Grande. Clara tried to bring more of the map into focus, but she lost her train of thought when she heard Matthew sputtering loudly.

Wasps were swarming all around him. They were so thick around Matthew's head that it appeared his hair was brown. Matthew thrashed his arms all around his head swatting the wasps. Their buzzing became so loud that its vibration sounded like the train running fast against the tracks. Clara stopped Flash and jumped down off him. She ran up to Raven's side and said quietly to Matthew, "Try not to swat at them, because you are only making them angry. I have an idea," she said, running back to Flash and pulling out the candle. She lit it and ran back to Matthew. She held the candle's burning wick up by his head. The wasps quickly began to disperse.

With the wasps gone, Clara snuffed the candle and held her hand up to Matthew. "Climb down, Matthew," she demanded.

Matthew pulled his foot from the stirrup and slowly brought his other leg over Raven's rump. He dropped to the ground and fell on his back. Clara quickly sat down beside him and lifted his head and laid it in her lap. His face had begun puffing up like a balloon from the stings. Small, red welts began growing into purplish colored mounds. His eyelids were thicker than his lips. She could just barely see the blueness of them through the tiny slits. "Matthew, I'll get some water and salve. Lie still. I'll be right back," Clara said gently laying his head on the ground.

She rushed to Flash and pulled off the canteen and then pulled the salve from the saddlebag. Clara felt her heart beating hard inside her small chest. Blood had rushed into her head and her breathing was quick and shallow. Her eye began twitching sporadically. She told herself to calm down and not to panic.

Clara put Matthew's head back in her lap when she returned. She tried to give him a drink, but he could hardly open his swollen mouth enough to get the canteen spout into his mouth. She poured water from the canteen onto his handkerchief that she had pulled from his neck. Clara bathed his face with the water. Her hands were so sweaty from fear that she couldn't get the small, tin can open. She rubbed her hands quickly against the ground and then rubbed them together drying them with the coarse sand. She grasped the bottom of the tin with one hand and then used the other to twist its cover counterclockwise. It opened with a loud popping snap.

Clara dipped her fingers deep into the thick salve and began rubbing the sticky substance all over Matthew's face and neck. She lifted his head and rubbed it on the back of his neck and behind his ears. He tried to mumble something to her, but she could not understand. Clara looked around them and knew she had to get him into some better shelter. She figured they had ridden about two hours from the waterfall. She decided that getting him back there was the best option she had.

Matthew's size posed a real problem. She could not lift him onto Raven. She tried to get him up, but he fell over as if he were a rag doll when she sat him up. She laid him back down on the ground and began looking for some long, thin sturdy branches. She found some sturdy green limbs hanging low enough to the ground for her to reach. With Matthew's long bladed knife, Clara cut and chopped at the branches until they broke off. With blistered hands, Clara laid them next to Matthew. Clara then took her lasso and began cutting it into pieces three feet long. After she had six pieces cut, she laid the long thin branches almost three feet apart. She took the lasso pieces and began tying one end on each thin branch. She made double thick knots the way Pete had taught her at the end of each rope. The *travois* looked like a ladder with rope rungs.

Clara pulled her bedroll down from Flash's back and rolled the blanket out over the top of the travois. She cut holes into the blanket's four corners and wrapped the blanket's corners tightly around the travois' corners and then securely tied them with shorter pieces of rope.

Clara then took Matthew's lasso and looped its center around her saddle horn twice. She took each end of the lasso and brought it through each stirrup of her saddle and to the rear of Flash. She lifted the travois and tied the lasso's ends securely to the ends of the thin branches. She backed Flash up toward Matthew, so that Matthew's head was almost touching the end of the travois. "Easy Boy. Slow now. It's okay," she said, softly and gently to Flash to keep him calm while she pulled Matthew onto the travois.

With her legs sprawled outward with a foot on each side of the travois, Clara stood at Matthew's head. She bent over and lifted his shoulders. She lodged her tiny, sore wrists under his armpits and grasped the front of his shoulders by digging her long, blistered fingers deeply into his flesh. Clara slowly began dragging Matthew onto the travois as she gradually walked backward, straddling the travois. Her back groaned with pain. All the muscles in her legs bulged from pulling Matthew's heavy weight. The veins in her neck popped out as she clenched her teeth and pulled him. The entire time she cooed and spoke softly to Flash to keep him from spooking from all the commotion going on behind him. With Matthew on the travois, she then took his blanket and covered him.

Perspiration dripped from Clara's face and she could feel it trickling inside her shirt between her shoulder blades. Her legs trembled with muscle spasms. She turned Flash around. With her free hand she grabbed Raven's reins. With bleeding, blistered hands, she led both horses back toward the waterfall. She walked over the uneven ground stumbling over rocks and large brush and tree roots. Her shoulders and back began aching much worse. Clara figured that Matthew must weigh close to two hundred pounds. She knew he was tall, but she didn't know how tall until she dragged him onto the travois. His large black boots hung over the end of the travois leaving strange markings on the ground between the tracks the thin limbs made.

Outbursts of groans and cries escaped Matthew as the travois bumped along the trail. Clara tried to be careful and avoid the really rough areas. It didn't seem to help, though. Matthew bounced up and down behind Flash. She took her time getting back to the waterfall. She stopped often and checked Matthew. He became feverish and thrashed his head back and forth, mumbling. Clara couldn't understand anything he said. She knew she had to do something, or he might die. Suddenly, winning the race wasn't important. Saving Matthew's life was the only concern she had now.

Chapter 28
Life or Death

Clara reached the waterfall early in the afternoon. The bright glaring sun had already begun sinking toward the west. Clara lay on her stomach beside the pond and cupped cold water through her dry cracked lips and into her mouth. She splashed the icy water all over her hot, sunburned face and rinsed the sweat from her neck with her hands.

She went to Matthew's side. The fever had intensified. When she touched him, his skin felt as hot as a fresh loaf of bread pulled from the oven. Clara knew she needed to cool him off to reduce his temperature. She figured the pool's water would be too cold and might cause more harm. She decided the best thing to do was to get him into the tunnel's hot spring. She tried again to get him to drink, but he didn't respond to her prodding.

Clara took Matthew's large knife from his saddlebag and began cutting the vines away from the tunnel's entrance. The vines ripped her skin open and scratched the backsides of her hands. Her blood mixed with the green grape juice. The scratches stung when the juice oozed into them, but she continued to work hard and fast. The juice made her hands sticky.

Once she had cut away enough vines to make room for Flash and the travois, Clara led Flash into the tunnel pulling Matthew behind him. After lighting a candle, Clara led Flash over to the side of the spring where the large granite rock was. She pulled Matthew's boots off first and then unbuckled his belt and pants. She lifted him up around the waist and tugged at his pants. With the waist of his pants down around his hips, she then took a pant leg in each hand and pulled them off him. She unbuttoned his shirt and carefully lifted one arm at a time and pulled them out of the sleeves. Stripped down to his long underwear, Matthew looked much smaller and paler.

Clara untied the lasso from the travois connected to the saddle horn. Afraid she wouldn't he able to hold him up in the water and he might drown, she took the ends of the lasso she untied from the travois and tied them under Matthew's arms and around his chest. She took off her breeches and stepped into the spring. Slowly she pulled Matthew in by his feet. She then grabbed his knees and pulled him farther in. Finally, she had his rump sitting on the granite seat. She got in behind him and laid his back up against her small chest. Clara slowly bathed Matthew with his handkerchief. She gently washed his battered and swollen face and neck.

Matthew moved his head slightly and tried to mumble, but she could not understand what he said to her. He reached up slowly with a very weak hand and squeezed her elbow as she sponged him. This gesture made Clara feel better. It meant he still knew what was going on. Clara and Matthew stayed in the warm ripples of the spring for an hour or more. Clara enjoyed the secure feeling the hot bubbling water gave her, as it massaged and tickled her skin with a smooth steady pace. Matthew had relaxed and fallen asleep lying against Clara. She continued to sponge him, and as she did, she hummed a lullaby her mother had sung to her as a child.

Reluctantly, Clara decided to get herself and Matthew out of the spring. She pulled herself up and sat on the edge of the spring and held Matthew's back between her legs. She put her arms under his and wrapped hers around his shoulders as tightly as she could. She tried to lift him, but it was impossible. She clicked her tongue toward Flash and said "Walk," quietly. Flash immediately obeyed. Clara and Flash slowly pulled Matthew from the spring. She told Flash to "Whoa," and he did instantly.

Clara untied the rope she had around Matthew's chest. She rolled Matthew's blanket up and put it under his head. Clara then untied hers from the makeshift travois and covered his legs with it. After pulling her breeches back on, she unsaddled Flash and led him back outside. Raven was grazing nearby and still saddled, too. Clara took his tack off and turned both horses loose to graze and drink. Before Flash went too far, she wrapped her arms around his huge, thick neck and kissed him gently as she thanked him for his help.

Clara turned toward the tunnel, and as she did, she noticed a clay pot painted with red stripes on it sitting by the opening. She picked up the pot and looked inside. There was a thick, sweet smelling substance in it. She dipped a finger into it. The moist mass was very warm. It stuck to her

166

finger as if it were mud. She brought her small finger up to her nose and inhaled. It was mud. She smelled the dirt and also a sweet fruity smell. She could see small pieces of leaves and berries cut up in the mud mixture. It had an oily film on the very top of it. Clara looked around to find the person who made the medicine, but she couldn't see him.

Clara walked inside the tunnel with the gift in her hand. She felt eerie knowing that somebody was out there watching her. But also she felt relieved that some other person was there to help with Matthew. She hadn't thought of making a *poultice* to put over the wounds to draw the wasps' venom out.

Matthew lay still where she had left him. She brought the candle close to his side. Clara could see the purplish red welts standing high on his red blotchy skin where the wasps had stung him. She carefully dipped her finger into the clay pot and slowly and gently packed the poultice on his face. She covered his entire face including his swollen eyes. The poultice stood about an inch above his swollen face. Clara then carefully wrapped Matthew's shirt around his head leaving a space open around his mouth and nose for him to breathe.

She picked up his pants and hung them over the saddle. As she did, something fell from the pocket. It was a piece of yellowed paper folded just like José's map. She unfolded the piece of paper and it was the map she had looked so hard for earlier. "Rotten scoundrel. You had my map the whole time," she whispered quietly in Matthew's direction. It didn't change her mood any, though.

She aimed to pull Matthew Miller through this fix
whether she liked him or not. She figured kindness
rather than bitterness would assist his healing much
quicker. Clara leaned back against Flash's saddle
and quickly slipped off to sleep.

She awakened suddenly to the sound of loud
moans and cries. As she opened her eyes, she saw
Matthew thrashing and kicking about. Clara
quickly crawled over to him on her hands and knees
and began to talk soothingly to him. "Matthew,
shush now. It's okay. I'm right here," she cooed as
she rocked his upper body gently in her cradled
arms. She pulled the shirt away from his face as it
had gotten tightly wrapped around him from his
thrashing. His face didn't appear to be as swollen as
it was earlier. He opened his lips and moaned,
"Wawawater."

Clara reached behind her and grabbed the
canteen. She lifted his head slightly with one hand
and tipped the canteen to his lips with the other. He
swallowed so hard it echoed inside the tunnel,
bouncing off its empty walls. He closed his lips
causing some water to spill on his neck and chest.
She wiped him off with her sleeve. "Matthew, I'm
so glad that you are coming around," she said,
smiling down at him.

He slowly brought his hand to his face and
touched it. She watched as his large, thick fingers
moved to his eyes and ran over the crusty, dried
poultice. He then moved his hand toward Clara and
touched her face gently. He cupped her small chin
in his large hand and gave it a gentle squeeze.
Clara was glad when his hand then dropped down,

before he could feel the tears running down her cheeks. She felt so relieved that she wanted to just sit there and cry like a baby, but she knew she couldn't.

The hunger pangs, digging deeply inside her belly, finally got the best of her early in the evening. She needed to get another candle from the supplies outside, too. She carefully laid Matthew's head back on the rolled blanket and stood up. Her legs were numb from being under his weight all that time, so she tapped her feet lightly to get the circulation moving in them again. Little pricks of pain shot through them as they began to come to life.

When she stepped outside the tunnel's entrance, Clara was surprised to see that the sun had set and the moon was shining brightly. The sight of the burning campfire really surprised her, though. For some strange reason, the large clay pot sitting beside the fire on some hot stones didn't surprise her at all. She walked over to it and put her nose close to the pot. It smelled just like the soup left for her when she had been fished out of the raging river. It had the strong smell of chicken broth. Her stomach began to growl when the salty, savory smell reached her.

Clara pulled a spoon out of the saddlebag and untied her handkerchief from around her neck to use as a pot holder. She slowly walked back toward the tunnel balancing the soup in one hand. Before she went inside, she waved with her free hand in all directions and loudly said, "Thank you for all of your help and wisdom."

Clara went to Matthew and sat down beside him. She washed the poultice off around his mouth, telling him she had some nice warm chicken broth for him. He managed a very slight smile. Clara rested the back of his head against her left shoulder. With him propped up almost in a sitting position, she began to slowly spoon the broth into his mouth. He swallowed the soup and opened his mouth for more. She was very hungry, as her stomach kept growling and reminding her. But she had to feed Matthew first. He needed to regain his strength to recover.

Matthew managed to eat almost half of the pot of broth before he finally mumbled, "Enough." Clara laid him back down beside her and then she lifted the pot to her lips and drank from it. The warm, strong, salty tasting chicken broth warmed her throat as it slid silently into her empty stomach. It echoed when it bounced in the emptiness. She found a dried, hard biscuit in her bag and cleaned the pot out with it. The juice softened the biscuit and it tasted delicious as she bit into the solid bread dough.

By the time Clara had finished her meager dinner, Matthew had fallen asleep. She blew out the candle and lay close to Matthew. Clara curled up next to him to share her blanket. She heard his deep breaths as he inhaled and exhaled. The rhythm of his breathing slowly lulled her into a deep sleep. Romantic dreams spun tomorrow's reality.

Chapter 29
Surprised Emotions

Early the next morning, Clara woke with a kink in her neck. She rolled her head from side to side and rotated it so her chin touched her upper chest. It didn't seem to help much. Matthew was still sleeping, so she decided to sit in the spring to see if that would help. She lit the candle and quickly undressed and climbed into the water. The hot, steamy water bubbled up into her face making her giggle. The gurgling rumble it made as it raced into her mouth tickled. Clara swam all around the spring moving her head from side to side as she did the overhand stroke. The movement seemed to work the kink out of her neck and relax her back muscles.

She sat on the large granite seat and listened to Matthew's rhythmic breathing. She looked at her blistered, scratched hands. She felt stupid for not putting her gloves on yesterday, but in her panicked state of mind she didn't think of it. "Oh well, my hands will heal," she whispered to herself.

"Clara, are you here?" she heard Matthew stammer quietly.

"Coming, Matthew," she replied, pulling herself from the spring.

Clara quickly pulled her clothes on and went to Matthew. He had rolled himself onto his side and was facing her. "How do you feel, Matthew?" she asked, touching his shoulder.

"Better. Would you, please, help me get this stuff off my face?" he asked, as if he were a little boy.

Clara dunked the handkerchief into the water and began washing Matthew's face. She could tell before getting the poultice washed off that the swelling had gone down. She tried not to wash too hard, as she was sure his face was tender and sore. Though he didn't let on that it hurt. After washing his entire face, except his eyes, she said, "I'm going to wash your eyes now, so be still and don't try to open them until I tell you to." Matthew nodded in agreement.

"Okay, now you can slowly open your eyes," she said.

Matthew slowly opened his left eye first and then his right. Clara saw the deep blue emerging like a wave erupting along the shore as he opened his eyes. She put her fingertips up to the side of his face and brought her face closer to his. Clara looked deeply into his eyes and felt the alarms going off in her head that she had entered a danger zone. She smiled at him and said, "Matthew can you see me?"

"If you are the beautiful angel with speckled green and blue eyes and soft, rosy cheeks looking at me, then yes, I can see you," he answered, lifting up both of his hands and holding her head in them.

"Oh! Matthew! You are all right," she cried allowing her tears to run freely down her face.

"Thanks to you, Clara, I'm alive," he said, pulling her small face down to his chest and caressing the back of her head.

172

Clara left her chin on his chest and cried freely. She couldn't stop herself. Once the bucket of tears spilled, she couldn't stop them. Matthew held her close to him and told her over and over how grateful he was to her for saving his life. Finally, with all her crying finished, Clara lifted her head and looked deeply into Matthew's eyes. She slowly lowered her face toward his and stretched out her lips until they gently met Matthew's. His warm, soft, damp lips wrapped around hers like a warm blanket on a cold winter morning. One large hand remained on the back of her head and the other now gently caressed her small back. Never before had Clara kissed a boy, and she had never dreamt that it could be this wonderful.

Knowing that it was improper behavior, Clara reluctantly lifted herself away from Matthew and smiled down at him. "I'll go get us something to eat," she whispered softly, pushing herself to her feet.

Matthew smiled up at her and reached for her dangling hand. "I think I can get up, Clara, if you'll help me," he said.

"Very well, Matthew," Clara said while she braced herself against his back and put her arms under his and lifted.

Matthew pushed with his feet against the tunnel floor and slowly rose until he was standing on his feet. Clara noticed him wobbling some, so she put his arm around her thin shoulders and wrapped her arm around his waist and helped him walk toward the entrance. The morning was new. The sun was just beginning to rise. Dew lightly

covered the ground. Clara helped Matthew sit
down on a large log by the fire ring.

After getting the fire going, Clara pulled the
coffee pot from the supply pack. When she slipped
her fingers under the pot, she felt something wet
and gooey on them. She reached back into the pack
and grasped the cold, wet, slimy item. To her
surprise, a large, freshly cleaned jackrabbit slipped
out of the opening. She didn't wonder about the
gift. She just accepted it from her secret friend.

*"I know it is more than a friend. God sent a
Guardian Angel to watch over me. Why did I ever
question if there was a God? I know now that he
exists and he loves me just the way I am,"* she
thought to herself as she filled the coffee pot with
water.

She put the coffee at the fire's edge and then
rigged up a skewer and hung the rabbit over the fire
to cook. "You are truly amazin', Clara. A rabbit,
too," Matthew said with a broad smile.

Clara accepted the compliment. She had no
intentions of ever telling anybody about her
Guardian Angel. Clara knew that, someday when
the circumstances were right, she would meet him.
She figured there were good reasons he kept
himself concealed. Clara planned to honor that
concealment.

After the meat had cooked long enough,
Clara dripped some water on some hard, dried
biscuits and then laid them on the warm rocks by
the fire. Strong, bitter coffee aroma mingled in the
air with the crisp, oily snapping of the rabbit meat.
The sun made its ascension into the orange,

feathery, fluffed sky. Clara served breakfast on dark blue tin plates from her and Matthew's supply packs.

As the hot coffee pushed the biscuit down Clara's throat, it landed deliciously in her grateful stomach. Clara picked up a piece of the meat and pulled off a chunk with her teeth. Strings of meat caught between her teeth. But the rest of the plump, hot, roasted meat was chewed completely.

"Matthew, are you up to leaving today?" she asked.

"I'm afraid not. But I want you to go on. You can still win the race if you ride straight through tonight and all day tomorrow," he replied.

"Matthew, I'm not leaving you here alone. Besides, winning the race meant an awful lot to you, I thought."

"It did and still does, Clara. But I ain't in any shape to be racing just now. I figure I'll need to come up with another way to keep our ranch," he said, wishing he hadn't when he saw the surprised look on Clara's face.

"Keeping your ranch! What do you mean?" she asked, loudly.

"It is just that taxes and some payments got behind with the droughts and all. I planned to win the race and use the money to pay it all off," he answered, embarrassed that she knew.

"Well, then I say you still need to follow through with your plan," she said reassuringly.

"Clara, why did you want to win this race so bad?" he asked.

"First, I need the money for Veterinary School. Secondly, I wanted to prove to my father, and you, and all men, for that matter, that women can do a lot more than they are given credit for."

"Your father can afford to send you to school, can't he?" Matthew asked.

"He could, if he wanted to. But, my father thinks that a girl being an Animal Doctor is as ridiculous as a girl riding in a race," she answered, frowning.

"Well, I disagree with your father, Clara, which I can't help...considering...Never mind. You just get your gear together and go win that race. Your dream is worth fightin' for."

"I won't go without you, Matthew. Who is going to take care of you?" Clara said loudly, standing up.

"I'll be fine. I'll be back to town in a few days. Now, you get your gear and get out of here!" he yelled.

"I'll go only on one condition. That is, if I win the race, I split half the winnings with you. No argument, or I don't go!" she yelled back at him.

"Clara, you are a hard one to argue with. I accept your conditions. Now, get movin'," Matthew replied, smiling up at her not realizing the dangerous hands he was sending her into.

Chapter 30
Captured

With Flash saddled and all her gear packed, Clara walked over to Matthew. She knelt down next to him and asked again if he was sure he would be all right. "I'm fine, Clara, now get moving. The day is wasting," he answered, holding her hand tenderly.

Clara put her hand on the side of his face and kissed his cheek and whispered, "I'll try my best to win that race for us, Matthew." She stood up and walked to Flash. Without looking back at Matthew, she pulled herself into the saddle and nudged Flash hard. He jumped into a full run instantly. Clara's hair flew behind her as if it were a choir robe caught in the wind. She followed the same trail that she and Matthew had taken the day before. She covered the rough, hardened ground much faster, though. She allowed Flash to run at his fastest speed. They had to make up for a lot of lost time, if they had a chance at winning the race. She had to get to the second check point as quickly as possible.

Within a few hours of hard riding, Clara found the landmark José had drawn on the map. The large, round slab of rock resting on a high, thin, towering pile of smaller rocks projected upward high enough to be seen for miles. Clara turned Flash south and headed toward the Río Grande. She figured she would make the check point within a few hours. From there, if she rode all night, she'd be back into town by late afternoon tomorrow.

Clara slowed Flash and put him into a steady gait. She figured they would reach the bottom of the mountain more safely if she slowed him now. Clara also knew she needed his speed once they reached flat ground along the river. Working her way down the mountainside proved to be a little harder than she figured. Finally, she climbed down from Flash and began leading him. The trees grew thicker than she had thought they would on this side.

Suddenly, she heard branches cracking and voices. Perhaps, she had come farther than she suspected and was close to the check point. She picked up her pace and began skipping downward. Flash suddenly reared up behind her. As she turned toward him, she saw a big, long haired, bearded man in a knee length coat grab out for Flash. She rushed forward and kicked at the man. He began to laugh as big arms wrapped around her from behind. Clara kicked back at his legs and wiggled and squirmed as hard as she could. "Let go of me this instant, or I'll scream!" she yelled.

"Oh, she is a feisty one, Job," the captor laughed and picked her up from the ground.

Clara bit his hand and bolted away from him. She ran as fast as she could upward. She hadn't gotten far, though, when another big, ugly man stood in her pathway and spread his arms out. He cackled like a chicken saying, "Come here little Chickadee, come to PaPa Brewster."

Clara darted around him. Just as she cleared his side, he put out his foot and she stumbled to the ground. She fell face first into a pile of damp, rotten leaves. She felt her arm smack against a tree as she began falling. The rough bark ripped her sleeve from her bloody, skinned elbow to her blistered hands. Before she could get up, he grabbed her arms and pulled them behind her back. He roughly twisted rope around her thin, sore wrists, and knotted it so tightly that she felt her fingers tingling.

Flash still reared upward. The men could not get close to him. Clara yelled, "Flash go get help!"

Flash immediately turned toward the bottom on the mountainside and swiftly ran down it, bucking and kicking up dirt and leaves as he left. "Go get help," one of the men mocked in a baby voice toward Clara.

"You'll be sorry you ever touched me when my father gets hold of you, you big, ugly pigs!" Clara yelled from the ground.

"Oh! Boy! Brothers, she has a big, mean daddy. We best run and hide," another mimicked.

"He's the sheriff and trust me, you will be sorry!" she seethed between clenched teeth.

"Hey, boys did you hear that? We have us the sheriff's kid. How lucky can we get? We'll hold her for ransom," Pa Brewster said and then burped grotesquely.

"Where we going hide the little Chickadee?" Simon asked.

"Down by the waterfall a few hours back," he answered, "Ain't nobody going to find us there."

"I'll write a note. Simon, you take the note and a chunk of her hair to the jail and tell her Pa to bring five thousand dollars by his self. You bring him to us at the waterfall," Pa Brewster said.

Simon pulled out a long bladed knife and walked up to Clara. He yanked her hair and cut off a large section of it. Clara squirmed and kicked out at him, but he pushed her over until she lay on her back. Clara struggled but couldn't get back up, so she rolled over onto her stomach and pulled her knees up to her chest and with her head she managed to push and wiggle her way back up into a sitting position.

"C'mon let's get moving while there's daylight," Pa Brewster yelled as he untied Clara's hands from her back while Job held her. Then he took his lasso and tied it around her wrists again in front of her. He got on his horse and held the other end of the lasso in his hand and gave it a yank, pulling Clara almost off her feet. "You can either walk or get dragged," he said punching his horse's gut with his boot heels. They had no idea that they were taking her back to Matthew.

Chapter 31
The Hide-Out

Clara's feet stung from the blisters on the bottoms of them. The hot sun burned violently with its fiery engine browning the earth and making it shimmer with heat. Clara felt as if she had become a part of the earth. Her skin felt hard and dry from the heat. Her throat had swollen from thirst. She had asked several times for a drink, but they just laughed and kept moving.

Clara slowed down from thirst and exhaustion. Pa Brewster yanked hard on the rope and her knees crashed hard against the ground. "Get up, or I'll drag you," he yelled.

"I can't. I'm too tired. I need a drink," she cried with a sore throat.

"Suit yourself," he said, as he began to move the horse and pulled Clara down to her stomach.

With her arms yanked up in front of her, it felt as if they got pulled from their sockets. She lifted her head, but her chin bounced against the ground and all the skin peeled off it. Blood trickled and spattered the moving ground beneath her. Her body beat against the earth. Every rock and grain of dirt rubbed deeply into her flesh. Her clothes ripped as the jagged stones slit at the material. "Stop, Stop!" she begged through sobs.

He stopped and bellowed, "Now, get up!"

Clara lowered her arms and with her left elbow she pushed herself onto her left side. She bent her knees and brought them up until they were parallel with her hips. Using her left elbow, she pushed herself up into a sitting position so that she sat on her left buttock and leg. With her arms still tied and twisting her forward, she put both elbows on the ground in front of her. With her right leg resting on top of the left leg, she twisted her hips until both knees were on the ground. With her elbows, Clara walked them backward until they touched her knees. With bent knees and her bottom sitting on her feet, Clara had the position she needed to use her back muscles to pull herself up. She buried her toes in the ground and pushed backward with her leg muscles until she stood again.

He punched his horse in the side and they began walking again. Clara recognized the path they were on. She feared for Matthew. She could do nothing to stop these men. She prayed that God would keep them both alive until her father could rescue them.

Hearing the waterfall around the bend, Clara knew the long walk would end soon. She didn't know what to expect when they turned the bend. Suddenly, she heard Matthew calling her name as he rushed toward her. Pa Brewster kicked him in the gut as he passed his horse. Matthew doubled over and grabbed his stomach, but he kept coming toward Clara. He reached out for her and pulled her close to his massive chest. "Clara, what is going on here?" he asked her, holding her tightly against him.

Before Clara could answer, Job yanked her away from Matthew. Pa Brewster stood on the ground next to all of them. "Well, what do we have here. Some little lovebirds?" he asked, in a cocky tone.

Job jabbed a gun in Matthew's back and told him to grab his little sweetheart's rope and go sit down under the big tree by the pool. Matthew took Clara's hands and led her toward the tree. As he walked past his saddlebag, he jumped sideways knocking her down behind him and grabbed for his rifle. Job shot and hit the edge of Matthew's hand, blowing a small chunk of meat from it. Clara screamed and reached for Matthew's hand. He pushed her away from him. It was too late, though, Job and Pa Brewster were on top of them. They wrestled Matthew to the ground and took his gun. Job slammed the butt of the gun deep into Matthew's gut and spat a big wad of spit down at him.

He kicked at Matthew yelling, "Get on over there boy by that tree, now, or I'll blow your head off."

They dragged Matthew and Clara to the tree and tied them together back to back. They then wrapped the rope around the tree and tied it. Clara watched as the littlest brother, who didn't say or do much, began gathering firewood. "Now, Luke, you keep an eye on them while we go out and hunt us some meat," Pa Brewster said to the small brother.

"But, Pa, what--ifs--they--tries--to--gets-- away?" he stuttered.

"Well, Boy, shoot them!" he laughed, turning to leave.

"Yes--sir!" he answered proudly.

With them gone, Clara quickly explained to Matthew what had happened. "I'm sorry, Matthew, I didn't know what to do other than get myself killed to stop them from bringing me here."

"It's okay, Clara. We'll get out of this fix. Don't you be worrying none, now," he quietly said.

"Luke, do you suppose I could have some water?" Clara asked with tears in her eyes.

"I expect," he said, bringing a canteen toward her. He lifted its spout to her lips and Clara drank in the cool water. It felt good rushing down her hot, parched throat. He offered Matthew some, too. He went back to the horses and began to unsaddle them. He tied them out so they could graze.

Clara, being exhausted physically and emotionally, leaned her head against Matthew's back and drifted into a nightmarish sleep.

Chapter 32
Simon's Message

Early the next afternoon, as the sheriff and the Rangers made new plans to catch the Brewster Brothers, Simon Brewster burst through the jail's door.

"I got something for the Sheriff. It's private," he said, grinning through broken teeth.

The sheriff walked to the back of the jail with Simon and read the note. Simon shoved the chunk of Clara's hair in the sheriff's face. Sheriff Browning looked deep into Simon's mud-brown eyes and said, "If anything happens to my daughter, you'll wish you never laid eyes on her."

"Well, Sheriff, if you want her back alive you better just get that money and come with me by yourself. You ain't to be telling nobody, specially those Rangers. You hear? If we ain't back to the hide-out by tomorrow night, your little Chickadee is going to be dead," he said, smiling and letting out hot, disgusting, stinking breath.

"I'll meet you at the saloon in an hour," the sheriff said, turning away from him.

Sheriff Browning walked up to the Ranger in charge and said, "I'm afraid I have an urgent family matter. Go on without me."

Sheriff Browning went to the bank and asked Lawrence if he could talk to him about an urgent private matter. He quickly explained the situation to Lawrence. "You know I don't have that kind of money, Lawrence. Will you loan me the money? I promise I'll get it back to you. You're my only hope, Lawrence," he pleaded, with tears in his eyes.

"Sheriff, the money is yours. I'll cover it, if I have to," Lawrence said, patting him on the back.

With the money in his saddlebag, Sheriff Browning raced home for a fresh horse. He asked Jake to saddle up Solid Gold for him as he strode quickly toward his bedroom. He pulled the strongbox from under his bed and with a swift movement he unlocked it. With shaking hands and tears rolling down his cheeks, Sheriff Browning took the strangely shaped stone dangling from the leather strap from the box and pulled it down over his head. Just before it hit his chest, he reached up and grabbed it and brought it to his lips and kissed it and whispered, "Please, Abigail, help me find our daughter safe."

Sheriff Browning raced outside. Jake had Solid Gold saddled for him. Sheriff Browning packed his rifle and canteens onto the horse. "Jake, I want you to go stay with Deputy Quill until I get back. Tell him I said it was an emergency."

Sheriff Browning raced back to town and met Simon Brewster in the saloon. "Let's get going," he demanded when he approached Simon.

Simon grinned and gulped down his mug of beer and led the way out of the saloon. The sheriff followed him, unaware of the unexplainable experience that he rode toward.

Chapter 33
The Rescue

The unnamed warrior had found Flash
racing around in circles near the waterfall. He had
decided that River Turtle must finish her Sacred
Mountain on her own. He had stayed behind to
watch the young, yellow haired boy. All of River
Turtle's belongings were still on the horse. The
unnamed warrior had begun searching the wisdom
of Great Spirit to find River Turtle. He had tied
some of the horse's mane and tail hairs together
with some of his. He had then slowly burned the
mixture of hairs. With smoke coming out of the
unusual incense, the unnamed warrior had brought
it to his face. He slowly waved his hand and
pushed the smoke up into his nostrils and inhaled
deeply. He cried the song of despair and clicked his
teeth. He closed his eyes and sat with his legs
crossed. He lifted his chin and let the sun sear his
cheeks. Finally, after many hours had passed, Great
Spirit gave the advice.

Great Spirit had told the unnamed warrior to
wait for River Turtle's father. Great Spirit told him
to take the sacred, marked horse down the
mountainside. When River Turtle's father comes,
he had to wound the messenger and take her father
to the land of wall waters.

Sheriff Browning had made Solid Gold run
fast. He had wasted no daylight riding hard toward
Clara. They only stopped briefly to water the
horses. Now in the darkness with just the

moonlight to guide their way, they walked toward the hide-out.

The sheriff's blood ran hot and fast as he thought of his daughter. He wondered why he hadn't listened to her. Why was he so gol-darned set in his ways? She had dreams that she wanted to share with him, but he had always cut her off, because he didn't believe in them. He had been so wrong. At first, when he had learned that she had entered the race, he decided he would deal with her harshly. Now, though, he knew it was more his fault than hers that she had come out here. Clara, his and Abigail's daughter, was the dearest thing to his heart. She had the ability and will power to be an animal doctor. What right did he have to deny her? My wife gave me a daughter and then a son out of our love and her love for life. Clara had that same zest for life as her mother had. He promised Abigail that night, riding toward Clara's captors, that he would never stand in her way again.

At dawn the sheriff broke Solid Gold back into a full run. Simon raced ahead of him leading the way. As they approached the entrance to the small, narrow canyon that led up the mountainside, the unnamed warrior watched them. Just before the lead horse entered the canyon, the unnamed warrior turned the big white, horse loose in front of him. Flash came racing down the canyon and reared when he saw the rider. He bounced up and down on his front feet and pawed in the air, snorting.

Simon's horse reared up from fright and threw Simon to the ground. The unnamed warrior jumped from behind the shrubbery and hit the big man with a large rock and knocked him out. The sheriff jumped down from Solid Gold and ran toward the men. "Hold up there, now, don't kill him. I need him for directions," he yelled at the strange looking man.

The sunlight caught the stone hanging from the sheriff's neck and it reflected brightly into the unnamed warrior's eyes. Light and warmth surged his soul as he surrendered to the memories of the woman seasons before. The unnamed warrior shook his head free of the memories, though, and pointed to Flash. He motioned with his hands for the sheriff to follow the horse. "The horse will take me there?" he asked.

The unnamed warrior nodded his head.

"Let's tie him up then and get on our way," the sheriff said, turning toward his horse.

When he turned back with the rope, the unnamed warrior had vanished. Sheriff Browning shook his head in disbelief and tied Simon to a nearby tree. He quickly got back on his horse and began to follow Flash. Flash raced through the canyon and rushed through the forest toward Clara.

Clara and Matthew sat tied to each other as they had been for almost three days. Clara's wrist hurt from the tight ropes. She had asked several times for them to loosen the ropes, but they had just laughed at her. Clara and Matthew had gotten very little to eat and drink. Matthew had talked with her about ranching and how much he loved it. She had talked about her dreams of being an animal doctor. They had done a lot of sleeping, too. The lack of food and water, Clara figured had made them sleepier than usual.

While Matthew slept last night, she overheard the Brewsters talking about how they were going to kill the sheriff and the two of them. They knew they had to, because the sheriff would never stop chasing them if he lived. Clara tried to think of a plan to escape, but it was impossible to move, being tied together and around the tree. She had tried making friends with Luke, the simple one, but all that had done was gotten them a little more food and water than they may have gotten otherwise. Clara had hoped to make Luke see how wrong this was.

The bright, yellow-orange sun began to set in the western sky. Clara became more scared. She knew her father was to arrive tonight. She had an awful feeling that none of them were going to come out of this alive. If only she would have let them kill her earlier, Matthew and her father wouldn't be involved now, she thought. "Matthew, I'm so sorry for all of this trouble," she whispered quietly.

"Be still, Clara. You didn't do anything wrong," he answered softly.

"Matthew, we are going to die, aren't we?" she asked crying.

"No, we are not. Quiet now. Get some rest," he said calmly.

Clara leaned her head against Matthew's back and closed her eyes. Her mind filled with all kinds of pictures. First, her beautiful mother came into view. Her reddish-blond hair and green eyes sparkling like diamonds. Oh, how she had missed her mother all these years! Her brother, Jake came bouncing into her mind's eye. He had been a good brother. Sometimes he acted like a real brat, but that's probably what brothers do best, she figured. Then her big, strong, square-jawed father came into focus. She guessed she had loved him the most. They often disagreed about many things, but Clara thought it was because he loved her as much as she did him. He had tried for years to be a mother and a father to her. He had old fashioned ideas about girls. That's where they had had most of their trouble. She only wished he would have tried to understand her dream. That was Clara's last thought as she drifted off to sleep.

The unnamed warrior crept slowly down toward the camp. He lay on his belly and slithered silently across the ground as if he were a snake. River Turtle's captors were drinking and making a lot of noise by the campfire. The unnamed warrior crawled toward River Turtle and the blond haired boy. He took his knife, made from buffalo bone, and cut the rope from the tree. He quietly slipped around the tree, hiding in the shadows of River Turtle and the boy. As they slept, he took his knife and drew a turtle on its back in the sand next to the small red painted, clay bowl. With one upward slice he cut through the ropes that held them captive. At the moment the ropes loosened Clara and Matthew woke up, but the unnamed warrior had disappeared.

"Clara, pretend we are still tied," Matthew whispered.

Clara looked down at her feet and saw the clay bowl and the odd drawing in the dirt. "It's the same shape as Flash's birthmark," she whispered. She cleared her mind and focused on the sand drawing. "Where does this come from?" she asked herself. She dug deeply into her memory for her hidden thoughts. She ran through the corridors of her mind and opened all the passageways searching for the answer. She extracted every buried memory, but still she could not identify the shape. She made herself shake off the eerie feeling this mystery caused her and said, "It's a message, Matthew. My father is near." She didn't reveal to him, though, that she knew it was her Guardian Angel that had released them.

"I don't see Luke around. Must be he came to his wits and cut us loose," Matthew whispered to Clara.

"Must be," Clara agreed, smiling and knowing better.

"I expect your father any time now. When he gets here, jump up and hide behind this tree."

"Why, what are you going to do?" she asked.

"I'm going to go for my gun and help him," Matthew said.

"Well, I'm not hiding behind a tree, Matthew Miller," she said frankly.

"Clara, don't start arguing with me now. Just do as I say," he said harshly.

"Don't you be bossing me. I can take care of myself and you too, for that matter," she sputtered.

"Clara, I know you're capable of taking care of yourself, but would you just, this time, not argue and do as you're asked?" he pleaded.

Just then Sheriff Browning came up behind the tree. "Clara and Matthew are you all right?" he asked.

"Father!" Clara almost yelled, but caught herself.

He brought a rifle around to Matthew and a pistol to Clara. "Don't give her a gun!" Matthew whispered loudly.

"She needs to protect herself," Sheriff Browning said.

"But, gol-darnit, Sheriff, she's a girl!" Matthew said.

"I know, Matthew. But she is capable of handling a gun. I taught her myself," he said.

"On the count of three come out shooting. Try not to kill them. Let's just wound them and take them alive if we can," Sheriff Browning said.

"Why? After what they have done to Clara they deserve to die. Besides, I thought you liked killing drunks!" Matthew sarcastically whispered, loudly.

"Matthew, let's settle this once and for all. During one of your father's drunken rages, he had wrongly accused your mother of being unfaithful to him. After he had beaten her, he went to the barn where the stranger had asked to sleep for the night. He then hanged the innocent man. Your mother had to run barefoot in her nightdress all the way to town for help. She feared that he would kill her, also. I tried everything possible to get him to come with me peacefully. But, he jumped me and we had a struggle over my gun. The gun went off, Matthew, and your father died instantly," Sheriff Browning recalled quietly.

"I never knew what happened, completely. Why didn't my mother tell me, Sheriff?"

"She didn't want you to have bad feelings about your father, Matthew. She had asked that I never tell what all had happened out there that night."

"Thank you for telling me, Sheriff. It's hard to swallow about your own father. But I reckon it's the downright truth."

The Brewster Brothers had gotten louder and were working their way toward Matthew and Clara. Suddenly Sheriff Browning yelled, "One, two, three!"

Clara lifted the pistol with both hands like her father had taught her. She held it away from her with outstretched arms that were level with her shoulders. She shot twice and then was knocked down from the back. She held the gun tight and pushed herself away from her assailant. Luke struggled to grab her again, but she kicked him in the gut. He stumbled backward and hit the ground. As she started to stand up, he got back on his feet and came at her again. Clara flung her arms around and hit him on the side of his head with the gun. Luke fell helplessly to the ground. When Clara whirled around to continue the battle, she realized the battle was over.

The Brewster Brothers lay on the ground moaning and groaning as her father and Matthew tied them up. She grabbed some rope and tied Luke up, too. With all of them securely tied, Clara rushed to her father. He picked her off the ground and hugged her so tightly that something dug deep into her chest. She looked down and saw the strange shaped stone.

"My mother's necklace," she said pointing to it.

"Yes, it is Clara," her father said as he lifted it over his head and placed it around her neck.

"My mother used to wear this all the time. When I was little I couldn't figure out the strange shape. Now, I can. It is a turtle on its back," she said, "And, Flash has the same mark on his neck, Father."

"I know, Clara," he nodded, with misty eyes.

"Father, where did my mother get this necklace?" Clara asked, puzzled over the strange feeling that crept silently inside her.

"Your mother had traveled by train as far as she could to join me in El Paso. She had to take the stage the rest of the way. The stage she rode was stopped by outlaws and robbed. They killed the driver and the men passengers. They took her for dead, too, and left her in the mountains. She did almost die until a stranger found her and took her higher into the mountains. There he nursed her broken spirits back to health. Although he had been very kind to her, she begged him to take her to town. He had to carry her all the way to El Paso, because her hip and leg had been broken. He had made the necklace and given it to her before he left her lying on the sidewalk in front of the jail one night. Your mother would never tell me any more about him. She had never revealed his heritage. She requested that if she died before you were eighteen, I was to keep the necklace and give it to you on your eighteenth birthday. I was to tell you that it had been a gift from her Guardian Angel and now that Guardian Angel was yours. I don't think she'll mind that I have given it to you a year early."

Clara held the stone between her fingers and felt the warmth that ran up her arm and into her heart. She felt a great rush of relief cross over her soul as she realized that she and her mother had shared the same Guardian Angel. Her mother would never be dead to her again. She lived inside this necklace and inside Clara's heart.

She called for Flash and he came running toward her. He stopped and greeted her in his usual way. On his hind legs with his front legs thrashing forward, he greeted his best friend. Clara ran to him with her arms spread wide open. She wrapped her arms around his enormous neck and kissed him on his soft muzzle.

Clara pulled herself up into the saddle and said, "I have a race to finish."

"Wait, Clara! Never mind," her father said, "go ahead and finish the race."

"Wait, Clara, I want to join you," Matthew said throwing his saddle on Raven.

"Matthew, you know we cannot win the race now. You should take it easy," she replied.

"I know we can't win, but let's finish it together," he said.

"Fine!" she said smiling, as she led the way out of the canyon, watched by her blood brother, the unnamed warrior.

Chapter 34
The Finish Line

Clara and Matthew rode hard all night and the entire next day. Clara had blisters on her hands from holding the reins for so long. She also had blisters on her bottom from the rock hard saddle, but she was not going to complain. The horses ran side by side. They were both frothy from sweat. Neither of them would give up the lead. They came running breathlessly into town late the next afternoon. The town folks who knew them cheered as they crossed the finish line. Mrs. Miller came rushing out of the shop to greet them.

Clara and Matthew jumped down from their horses at the same time and all three of them hugged in the street. She inquired about the sheriff. After they told her that he was fine, she announced there would be a celebration dinner at the ranch tomorrow evening.

Clara and Matthew said polite, proper good-byes and rushed toward their homes. Clara yelled for Jake as she walked up the lane. He came rushing out of the house and flung his small arms around her. She held him tight to her. Deputy Quill stood on the porch smiling. He offered to take care of Flash for Clara. She didn't argue.

Late that night as she lay in her bed, she thought of all she had gone through. She had learned many things, but most of all she knew she was capable of most anything she put her mind to. But she had, also, learned that she needed help along the way. It doesn't make one weak to take the help of others. It shows great strength to know your own limitations. She fell asleep thinking about her and her mother's Guardian Angel and wondering when she would meet him face to face. She looked forward to the day that she could touch the person who had touched her and her mother's spirits.

The next evening at Mrs. Miller's, Sheriff Browning informed Matthew and Clara that there was a three thousand dollar reward for the Brewster Brothers. "I can't collect it, because I'm a law man. And really since the two of you pretty much handled catching them on your own, you'll be sent the money from the Federal Marshal's office next week."

"Clara, I almost forgot to tell you. I ran into José today. He said to tell you the plan worked. What does that mean?" Matthew asked.

"It means José isn't the stable boy anymore at the Wilkinson's ranch," she replied smiling.

"Sheriff Browning, about my father and the terrible way I have behaved. Well, I want to apologize. I realized after seeing you in action up in those mountains, that you would never take a man's life if you didn't have to. I'll never question your judgment again," Matthew said, looking straight at the sheriff.

Sheriff Browning reached over and squeezed Matthew's arm and said, "Thank you, Son."

"Are you going to split the money evenly?" Jake asked, looking at Clara and Matthew.

"Well..." Matthew said.

"Well, what, Matthew Miller. You know darned well I deserve just as much of the money as you do. And, if you think for one minute that you are going to cheat me out of one red cent, you better just think again...."

Sheriff Browning quietly shut the door behind him and Mrs. Miller as they stepped out on to the long porch and listened to the first of many arguments between Clara and Matthew.

UNNAMED WARRIOR
Book 2 of The Clara Browning Series

EXCEPT

Clara saw his face grimace with intense pain. "John, is there anything I can do to help ease the pain?" she asked.

"It may help if I can lean back and relax," he answered.

After Clara banked the fire, she sat down next to him and slowly pulled her trunk in behind him. She braced herself against the saddle and helped him slide downward until he was almost lying. She gently pulled his head against her shoulder. Using her free hand she pulled the blanket over both of them. As she put her head against the saddle, she looked up into the star filled sky.

"Clara, do you believe in destiny?" John asked her quietly.

"I guess I do," she answered softly.

"I believe we were meant to be alone together like this," he whispered.

"Why's that?" she asked surprised.

"So that I could tell you how I feel about you," he answered.

"How you feel about me?" she asked nervously, remembering what he had said earlier when he was semiconscious.

"I've never felt this way before. You make me feel...."

"Hush!" she said, stretching her head over his.

"What? What is it?" he asked in a whisper.

"There's something out there," she responded, keeping her voice low as she reached for her rifle.

Matthew's heart spiraled downward with heavy pain when he saw Clara and John clinging to each other. Tears caught in his throat as he watched her holding John. All those feelings that had raced inside him came crashing to an end. He had felt so much for her. He had almost fooled himself into believing that she may have felt the same way toward him. He should have known better. She had avoided him like the plague all summer. Instantly, bitterness and anger replaced the love he had carried for her. If only he could make her feel the same pain he felt this moment, it would lessen his.

"Who's there?" Clara called out, raising the rifle toward the noise.

"Put the gun down, Clara!" Matthew sputtered as he moved toward her.

"Matthew Miller! Is that you?" she asked, surprised.

"Well, it's not your Guardian Angel," he answered sarcastically.

For the first time tonight, Clara thought of her shadow brother. Did Matthew somehow know about him, or was his statement just a fluke? "What are you doing up here?" she asked curiously.

"Looking for the two of you. Pete was real worried that something terrible had happened. Guess he shouldn't have bothered. Looks like you lovebirds just wanted some time alone," he growled angrily.

"Matthew, you're such an idiot!" Clara yelled, lowering John onto the saddle.

"Maybe a fool, Clara Browning, for risking my neck to come looking for you," he shouted.

Clara slowly walked toward Matthew. As she stood in front of him glaring, she lowered her voice and said calmly, "You can be so stupid sometimes. For your information, John is seriously hurt. I didn't dare take him any farther tonight. You do remember what it is like being hurt and needing help, don't you?"

Matthew thought back to the wasp stings and how Clara helped him pull through it. He also remembered that was when he fell in love with her. Remembering her kiss made his heart jolt. He also realized that perhaps John had fallen in love with her too. "I'm sorry. It's just that the two of you were all cozy together, and I thought...."

"Well don't think, Matthew. It's when you think that you get into trouble," Clara interrupted.

"Calm down!"

"I'll not calm down. You make me so mad! You come sneaking around my camp in the dark and then conjure up all kinds of crazy ideas about John and me in that sick mind of yours! Get out of here. I'll bring John in tomorrow myself!" she cried, turning around.

Matthew reached out and grabbed her hand and stepped toward her. He turned her to face him and held her gently by the shoulders. "I'm sorry, Clara. I shouldn't have come in unannounced. It was wrong of me to think anything about you and John. I'll stay the night and help you get him to camp in the morning."

Confused with her sudden feelings of warmth toward Matthew, Clara looked into his deep blue eyes and watched herself nod in agreement. She had to hold herself back from standing on her tiptoes and reaching for his lips with hers. How he confused her! One minute she wanted to belt him and the next minute she wanted to kiss him.

"Excuse me! If I can say something here, I'm capable of taking care of myself," John called, realizing that he had seen a highly combustible flame ignite in Clara for Matthew. That flame was meant for him. There was no way he was going to allow Matthew to steal it from him.

"Don't be silly, John. You can't make it back to camp alone. Now just everybody settle down and get some rest," Clara soothed, like a mother.

Matthew tied Raven to a nearby tree and took off his gear. He tossed his saddle down next to John. "If you need a sturdy shoulder to lean against, mines more fittin' than Clara's," he said.

Lowering his head against Clara's saddle, John shook his head and declined. Clara lay on the other side of John. She rolled onto her side and put both of them behind her. Her mind swirled with all that had been said and felt tonight with both John and Matthew. What was John driving at before Matthew came? Destiny and how he felt toward her. What about how confused she was when she saw Matthew? She wouldn't let him know that when she heard his voice her heart leapt into her throat. It didn't matter. Matthew did not care about her one bit, not the way she wanted him to care. "No! I don't want him to feel that way toward me," she scolded herself. "Besides, he's not near the gentleman that John is. Oh! But how do I feel about John? Go to sleep, Clara!" she shouted inside her head.

Unnamed Warrior quietly crawled toward Clara as she slept. He had to speak with her and this may be the only opportunity he would get to be alone with her. Slowly he placed his hand over her mouth.

Clara awakened, gasping for air. She opened her eyes and saw her shadow brother leaning over her. She reached up and patted his hand that cupped her mouth. He nodded and lifted his hand. He motioned for her to follow him quietly. She looked over her shoulder at John and Matthew, knowing she would not see them again for a long time.

COMING SOON

UNNAMED WARRIOR
BOOK TWO OF THE
CLARA BROWNING SERIES
PROJECTED RELEASE DATE
NOVEMBER 15, 2000

IOWA PASSAGE
BOOK THREE OF THE
CLARA BROWNING SERIES
PROJECTED RELEASE DATE
FEBRUARY 14, 2001

ADVANCE ORDERS AVAILABLE
BY CALLING COUNTRY HOME PUBLISHERS
AT 616-954-7634 OR FAXING
616-954-7633
OR
WRITING
COUNTRY HOME PUBLISHERS
6812 OLD 28TH ST., SE
SUITE "J"
GRAND RAPIDS, MI 49546
**RESERVE YOUR COPY TODAY FIRST 1000
COPIES SOLD OF BOOK TWO AND THREE
RECEIVE, FREE, A SPECIAL GIFT FROM
CYNDI HARPER-DEITERS**

Glossary

Apache. The generic name for Indians of the Athabasean linguistic stock. Archaeological evidence shows the first Apache bands came to the southwest in A.D. 825.

Bosque. Jungle-like area along the banks of the Río Grande.

Butterfield Southern Route. 1858 overland route set for Transcontinental Stage Line that ran through the Southwest from El Paso to Los Angeles.

Carson. Colonel Christopher "Kit" Carson, during the Civil War (1861-1865), used an army of volunteers to force the Mescalaro Apaches from their homes and relocated them at the Bosque Redundo Reservation of eastern New Mexico.

Digging Stick. A stick about 3 feet long stripped of its bark and has a sharpened point on the end. It enabled Native Americans to pry and lift the many edible plant roots.

Fetish. An object embracing a spirit that grants supernatural assistance if regarded with proper respect. If the owner believes it is a fetish, it is. If there is no belief in the fetish, then it is only a carving.

Geronimo. Chiricahua leader that negotiated a surrender with General George Crook on May 20, 1883. Geronimo agreed that he would return to the San Carlos reservation with his people within two months. He returned in March of 1884. He drove in 350 head of cattle, which he proposed to use for trading on the San Carlos Reservation. The authorities took his cattle. Geronimo felt this was an injustice and fled the reservation in 1885. He surrendered for the last time in September 1886 to General Miles.

Horsemint. Square stemmed member of the mint family. It reduces the pain and itching of insect bites by rubbing the crumbled leaves on the bites.

Medicine Pouch. A small leather pouch, usually worn around the neck. The owner kept his or her special treasures inside it that told of their life journey. In addition to treasures, healing natural remedies, such as herbs and roots, were kept inside. Some Native American tribes kept remedies inside their pouch that they felt brought protection and good luck to the owner.

Mescal. Also called Agave or Century Plant. It was a major food for the Southwestern Native Americans. The center stalk is edible when cooked. The plant's crown, flowers, and seeds were also eaten. The liquids from the flowers become a sweet, nonalcoholic drink. The juice of the leaves or raw plant can cause serious illness.

Mescalero Apache. A Southwestern Native American tribe named after a kind of cactus important in the Apache diet, **mescal**. They were master basket makers. During the Civil War, Mescaleros carried out raids on travelers near the El Paso end of the Butterfield Southern Route.

Mescalero Apache Indian Reservation. Located in southeastern New Mexico at the foot of the Sacramento and White Mountains. It was opened on May 27, 1873 by executive order of President Grant. Lipan and Chiricahua bands live on the Reservation with the Mescaleros.

Mt. Franklin. Elevation 6186 feet above sea level. This mountain range splits El Paso, Texas almost in half. The grays of the mountains remind us of the ancient inland sea. The red in the mountains tell the tale of lava surging up from long ago volcanoes.

Poultice. Soft moist bandages made of skunk cabbage leaves, the inner bark of slipper elm, and crushed roots of the cattail.

Quiver. A long case used to carry bow (approximately 3 feet long) and arrows (approximately 2 feet long). Most quivers could hold up to 100 arrows. Quivers were often made of animal skins and had shoulder straps for easier carrying.

Rawhide Thongs. String or rope made from animal skin to tie things together.

Southern Pacific Railroad. Four railroads: **Southern Pacific Railroad**, Santa Fe Railroad, The Texas & Pacific Railroad, and The Galveston, Harrisburg & San Antonio Railroad, raced into El Paso, Texas in 1881. **Southern Pacific Railroad** arrived first, May 13, 1881; however, May 31, 1881 is widely recognized as the date the first engine "came down the line". From California into Yuma, Arizona, it then stretched 560 miles across the Arizona and New Mexico deserts to reach El Paso, Texas.

Steaming Pit. A pit dug in the ground and lined with stones. A fire is then built in it. After the fire burns down to coals, they are scraped out and a layer of wet grass is placed over the hot stones. The food is placed on the grass and covered with more wet grass. Water is poured on the food. When the water reaches the hot stones, steam forms. The pit is quickly covered with flat rocks or animal hide and then buried with dirt to seal the steam. After several hours, the food is cooked.

Travois. A flat bed-like carrier pulled behind a horse or dog to move belongings from one camp to the next, or to move a sick person.

Turtle Creation. Many Apaches believed that the turtle brought the earth up from under the water.

Ussen or Yuson. Many Apache tribes considered Ussen the giver of life, the most powerful of the supernatural beings.

Vision Quest. A custom of some Native American tribes. At the approximate age of twelve years or more, the youngster takes a solitary trip to find a purpose and guide in life. Usually sent out with no food or water, the child waits for a vision to come. The vision brings the youngster a spirit helper for life. The spirit helper may be as an animal or person.

White Sands. At the northern end of the Chihuahuan Desert lies a dry ocean of Granular Gypsum near Alamogordo, New Mexico. The San Andres Mountains are on the west side of the White Sands and the Sacramento Mountains are on the east side.

Wickiups. Mescalaro Apache Indians' homes. A wickiups requires twenty wooden sticks with natural forks in them. The sticks are placed so they all lean toward each other. It is topped with tree boughs that are woven into place and then covered with bark, grass, and reeds.

BIBLIOGRAPHY

Cremony, J. C., *Life Among the Apaches,* Texas:
Rio Grand Press, 1970.

Liptak Karen, *North American Indian Survival
Skills*, New York: Franklin Watts, 1990.

Lockwood, Frank C., *The Apache Indians*, New
York: Macmillan, 1938.

Mails, Thomas E., *The People Called Apache*, N.J
Prentice-Hall, 1974.

McNeer, May and Lynd Ward, *The American Indian
Story*, New York: Ariel Books, 1963.

Ogle, Ralph Hendrick, *Federal Control of the
Western Apaches 1848-1886*, New Mexico:
University of New Mexico Press, 1970.

Opler, Morris E., *An Apache Life-Way*, Cooper
Square Publishers, 1965.

*Encyclopedia Americana, Volume 2, US
Constitution Bicentennial Commemorative Edition-
Connecticut: Groiler, Inc., 1989.*

*The Historical Encyclopedia of Texas, Volume 1.
By: The Texas Historical Society; Ellis Arthur
Davis, Editor.*

HOW TO ORDER CLARA BROWNING
BOOKS BY CYNDI HARPER-DEITERS

CALL COUNTRY HOME PUBLISHERS AT
(616) 954-7634 OR FAX YOUR ORDER
(ORDER FORM ATTACHED) TO:
(616)- 954-7633 OR VISIT CYNDI'S WEBSITE

RIVER TURTLE
**$8.95 PLUS $2.50 FOR S&H
FIRST 2000 BOOKS SOLD INCLUDE, FREE,
A HAND CARVED, STONE TURTLE
NECKLACE, A SPECIAL GIFT FROM
THE AUTHOR, CYNDI HARPER-DEITERS.**

UNNAMED WARRIOR
**$8.95 PLUS $2.50 FOR S&H
FIRST 1000 BOOKS SOLD INCLUDE, FREE,
A HAND CRAFTED, LEATHER, MEDICINE
POUCH, A SPECIAL GIFT FROM
THE AUTHOR, CYNDI HARPER-DEITERS.**

IOWA PASSAGE
**$8.95 PLUS $2.50 FOR S&H
FIRST 1000 BOOKS SOLD INCLUDE, FREE,
A HAND CARVED, WOODEN AND BEADED
BRACELET, A SPECIAL GIFT FROM
THE AUTHOR, CYNDI HARPER-DEITERS.**

ORDER FORM

RIVER TURTLE (R/D 10-15-2000)
HOW MANY COPIES?_____ @ $8.95
EACH PLUS $2.50 EACH S&H

UNNAMED WARRIOR (11-15-2000) PROJECTED
HOW MANY COPIES?_____ @ $8.95
EACH PLUS $2.50 EACH S&H

IOWA PASSAGE (R/D 02-14-2001) PROJECTED
HOW MANY COPIES?_____ @ $8.95
EACH PLUS $2.50 EACH S&H

WOULD YOU LIKE YOUR BOOK(S)
AUTHOGRAPHED & PERSONALIZED?
TO WHOM:_____

SHIP BOOK(S) TO:

_____
NAME

_____
MAILING ADDRESS

_____
STATE   ZIP
PHONE NUMBER(_____)_____-_____
MAIL WITH CHECK PAYABLE TO:
COUNTRY HOME PUBLISHERS
6812 OLD 28TH ST., S.E., SUITE "J"
GRAND RAPIDS, MI 49546
OR FAX TO (616) 954-7633 OR CALL 954-7634

ORDER FORM

JONATHAN MICHAEL BOOKS

ALL BOOKS RETAIL FOR $4.95 EACH PLUS $1.75 PER BOOK SHIPPING & HANDLING

JONATHAN MICHAEL THE RESIDENT ROOSTER
HOW MANY?_____

JONATHAN MICHAEL AND THE UNINVITED GUEST
HOW MANY?_____

JONATHAN MICHAEL AND MOTHER NATURE'S FURY
HOW MANY?_____

JONATHAN MICHAEL AND THE PERILOUS FLIGHT
HOW MANY?_____

JONATHAN MICHAEL AND THE PICKED POCKET
HOW MANY?_____

JONAHTAN MICHAEL AND THE TWISTED TALE
HOW MANY?_____

JONATHAN MICHAEL AND THE FOREST FLOOR PROMISE
HOW MANY?_____

JONATHAN MICHAEL AND THE LANGUAGE TRAP
HOW MANY?_____

WOULD YOU LIKE YOUR BOOK(S) AUTOGRAPHED & PERSONALIZED?
TO WHOM:_____

SHIP BOOK(S) TO:

_____
NAME

_____
MAILING ADDRESS

_____
STATE   ZIP
PHONE NUMBER(_____)_____-_____MAIL
MAIL TO:COUNTRY HOME PUBLISHERS:
6812 OLD 28TH ST., SE SUITE "J" GRAND RAPIDS, MI 49546 OR FAX TO (616) 954-7633 OR CALL 954-7634

ABOUT THE AUTHOR

Cyndi Harper-Deiters is an award-winning children's author and a graduate of the Institute of Children's Literature. She has three daughters, two dogs, two cats, and two birds. When Cyndi is not traveling and speaking in schools, she is spending her time reading and writing from her fabulous and most stunning Michigan gardens, which were designed and created by her fiancée, Mustapha Tamim.